I0452423

To Amy

For your constant enthusiasm. What started as a one-off, dieselpunk Christmas series in space turned into a whole universe.

The Isle of Skye
Book One

This is a work of fiction. Names, characters, businesses, places, events, locales, and incidents are either the products of the author's imagination or used in a fictitious manner. Any resemblance to actual persons, living or dead, or actual events is purely coincidental.

ISBN: 979-8-9897322-1-0

© 2024 by Josh Bouchard, all rights reserved
Cover art and *Isle of Skye* design by Gus Amaral
(Instagram: @mr.goose_art)

Chapters

1. Gideon, The Captain

Gideon buys himself a lever-action katana for Christmas.

Gideon walked through the promenade, looking for his favored gunsmith. He stroked a hand through his thick hair and opened his black trench coat. Stations usually ran cold. This one ran hot.

He found the shop and strolled inside, smirking at all the Christmas decorations on display. They were a pleasant distraction from the station's industrial aesthetic.

"Hey! Welcome!" a North American accent called out. A middle-aged, lanky gentleman in thick glasses and a work apron emerged. "You're Gideon, right?" he asked, extending a hand.

"Yes. Good to see you again, James." He looked around the shop. "Funny, even out here you blokes don't forget about Christmas."

"Of course not! We're still on Earth's calendar," James said. "Now, what can I help you with?"

"Well," Gideon said. "I'm in the market for a revolver and a melee weapon."

"Let's start with the revolver," James said, leading Gideon to a glass cabinet. "See anything you like?"

"Yes," Gideon said. "Is that a Remy-Larsson?"

"It sure is," James said, opening the case and picking up the oversized revolver. "The Remy-Larsson twin-cylinder auto-revolver, to be precise. Fires the classic .457 cartridge, but with a Gauss accelerator built into the barrel. Holds twelve rounds between the two cylinders."

Gideon spun the two cylinders, making sure the revolver was clear.

"Wanna give it a try on the range?" James asked.

"You have a range here? On the station?" Gideon asked.

"Of course! Come on back." James led the way to the back of the shop and through a door where a short, single aisle range had been set up. Beat-up targets and sandbags littered the range, and the backstop was badly pockmarked, but it was sturdy.

James put a couple moon-clips of rounds on the table. "Go ahead. Load up and pop off a clip," he said to Gideon. "Oh, you've got aural implants, right?"

"Oh yes," Gideon confirmed. He loaded the clip into one of the cylinders, brought the revolver to sights, pulled back the hammer, and fired. A sandbag exploded, but the round continued on and buried itself in the backstop.

He pulled off a few more rounds to get a feel for it. Had it not been for their aural implants, their eardrums would've been shattered.

"Kicks, doesn't it!" James said. "Beautiful piece of French and Nordic engineering. It does have an optional compensator I can install, which makes it too big for the holster, but I can 3D print you a new one in about two minutes."

"I'll take it," Gideon said. He opened the cylinder and removed the clip.

"Wonderful!" James said. "Now, come on back into the shop. You said you're looking for a melee weapon of some kind? You need sharp or blunt?"

"Sharp," Gideon said.

"All right," James said, leading them to his section of bladed weapons. "I find blades are like guns. Really depends what you like, what it's for. Let me know what catches your eye."

"Tell me about that machete," Gideon said.

"Yes. That's a Camara brand. Diesel-powered to give you that extra swing. Has a tungsten-alloy edge that'll cut through just about anything organic."

"Hmm, not quite what I'm looking for," Gideon said, stroking his short beard. "Need something more powerful."

"Well, if it's power you're looking for, I've got a Diesel-powered claymore right over here," James said.

"Now you're speaking the language of my people," Gideon said with glee. "Why is everything diesel-powered here, anyway?"

"I mean, you know," James said. "We orbit Titan, and all they do is make every oil distillate possible. I mean the station's backup generators run on diesel, we got so much of the stuff." He helped Gideon strap on the massive Scottish claymore, and fired up the engine.
Gideon gave it a few awkward practice swings.

"The two-stroke engine is great!" James shouted over the roar of the diesel engine.

"What?" Gideon shouted back.

"I SAID THE TWO-STROKE ENGINE IS GREAT! SEE HOW YOU CAN SWING THAT THING ONE-HANDED?"

Gideon was pleased, but shut it down. "I like it," he said. "But it's a bit unwieldy, and a wee bit loud. You have something quiet? Something with finesse?"

James thought for a moment. "I think I have exactly what you're looking for." He went to the wall and took down an elegant sword.

"Ooooo," Gideon said. "Do tell me about that beauty."

"This," James said, placing the blade on the cabinet in front of Gideon. "Is the Stetson-Takahashi lever-action katana. American welding meets Japanese tradition. The blade is hand-forged in the traditional manner by the Takahashi school, so it's a proper katana. It's treated with a liquid diamond coating, then lined with a plasma filament along the edge."

Gideon lifted the sword with reverence. He pulled the weapon part way from its scabbard, exposing the blade. "What powers it?" he asked.

"Your standard plasma-cutting cartridge," James said. "The handle holds eight total. Each cartridge is good for about three or four cuts, depending on what you're slicing through."

"Will it cut through diamond-weave Kevlar?" Gideon asked.

"Oh yeah," James said. "That thing will cut clear through a bulkhead. A couple of the welding guys stationed here even bought one. They go through plasma cartridges quickly, but nothing cuts faster."

"And the lever? Just rack it like this?"

"Yup. Works just like your classic lever-action rifle. Racking the lever clears the spent cartridge and loads a fresh one. Wanna try it out?"

"Would love to," Gideon said. They made their way to a corner of the shop where a slagged, scrap bulkhead sat.

"Here," James said, handing him a pair of auto-shading goggles. "The plasma arc only activates when you make contact with something, but man is it bright."

"Thank you." Gideon put the goggles on and loaded the katana with a couple plasma cartridges. He racked the lever, held the trigger, and swung for the bulkhead.

The katana cut through it like softened butter.

"Power, finesse, and best of all, it's quiet," James said.

Gideon looked over the blade. "Is this the indicator? On the guard?"

"Yup. Tells you how much charge is left on that cartridge. You'll get used to it with practice. Say you got about two swings left on that one."

Gideon readied up and threw two more cuts. He racked the lever again. The spent cartridge went flying and was replaced with a fresh one. He pulled the trigger again, and cut the bulkhead straight down the middle, cleaving it in half.

"A work of art, isn't it!" James said. "See how that last cut was a lot longer? You cut through about four feet of mild steel there. That cartridge is probably spent."

Gideon checked the indicator. The cartridge was spent. He racked the lever again, clearing the blade. "I'll take it," he said, sheathing it and returning it to James.

"Wonderful! Just the Remy-Larsson and the katana then? You set on rifles, shotguns, particle beams, ammo?"

"No, thank you. I'm good on those. Just the katana and the revolver."

"And did you want the compensator on the Remy-Larsson and for me to print up a new holster?"

"No, but thank you."

"Perfect, let me ring you up." James led the way to his touchpad. He queued up the cost. "And since it's Christmas, let me throw in a few boxes of the plasma cartridges and those .457s. On me."

"That's appreciated, mate. You don't have to do that."

James waved it off. "Please. It's nothing." He turned the touchpad towards Gideon.

"Woo, look at the price on that blade," Gideon said. "You said a couple welders bought their own?" He touched his phone to the pad, initiating the transaction.

"You know how much welders out here make? They can get stationed here for six months then head back to Earth and not work for the next five years."

Gideon was impressed. "I should've been a welder."

"Let me package all this up and send it your way," James said. "Where are you docked?"

"Concourse A, port 17."

"A17," James echoed. "You'll get it before dinner. And your ship is the *Isle of Skye,* right?"

"You remembered! Thanks again, James."

"Hey, my pleasure. Thanks for always stopping in when you're here."

Gideon fanned his trench coat again. "What's going on with the station? I don't remember it being so hot."

"Oh, some ventilation problems. Usually the vents dump the excess reactor heat, but half of them went offline yesterday. They're fixing them."

"Too bad. Anyway, thanks again."

"You bet! Merry Christmas!"

"And Merry Christmas to you, mate." Gideon left the shop and strolled back out on the promenade. The rest of his crew would still be busy running their own errands. With Christmas on his mind, he made his way to the cafeteria, wondering if he could scavenge together a Christmas dinner for them.

2. Kiwi, The Rosevine

Kiwi discovers Twin Diesel bourbon.

Kiwi plopped all 93-pounds of her tiny frame onto the barstool. She dropped her gear bag to the floor, and winced when her long, raven-black hair got caught in the straps.

"Hey, good afternoon," a female bartender said. "What can I get started for ya?"

Kiwi was used to getting chided for looking too young to drink, but Gideon had been right; this station just didn't care.

"Hey there," she said back. She thought about waiting for a random guy to come up and buy her a drink, but the bar was empty and she wasn't feeling patient. "Can I get a half-pint of whatever you have on tap, and a whiskey straight up?"

"Of course," the bartender said, pulling her short, blonde hair behind her ears, grabbing a glass, and pulling the beer tap. "I like your tatts, by the way. They're really cute."

"Oh, thank you," Kiwi said. She wore a tank top and shorts, which put her tattoo on full display: a vibrant rose vine that started at her left hand, snaked up to her shoulder, flowed down her back, wrapped around her right leg, and ended at her ankle.

The bartender served the beer.

"Cool, thanks." Kiwi took a gulp. "This is good. A little sweet, but I like it."

"Yeah, that's our 'Two-Stroke' lager that we make here," the bartender said, serving up a generous pour of whiskey. "Same with this. We get a bunch of corn from the bio-domes down on Titan, so a few of the welders here slapped together a still, and before you know it we've got our own station's bourbon."

Kiwi downed half of the measure. Some of it got into her windpipe. She started hacking.

The bartender couldn't help a giggle. "Good stuff, isn't it?"

Kiwi nodded, wiping a combination of bourbon and spittle from her mouth. "It's smooth when it doesn't get into your lungs," she managed to say. The whiskey in her throat made her voice even huskier than it already was. "This stuff have a label? It's great."

"Oh yeah," the bartender said, producing the bottle. "They've made a nice business out of it."

Kiwi read the label. "Ha! 'Twin Diesel Bourbon.' Great name."

"I know, right?" the bartender said. "I love the engine design on the label."

"Yeah, that's a diesel engine," Kiwi said. "I grew up on a farm. I've been fixing diesel engines since I was a kid."

"Oh yeah?" the bartender said. "Whereabouts you from?"

"Wisconsin," Kiwi said.

The bartender nodded. "I knew I heard a little Midwest in you. I'm from Chicago, myself."

"That practically makes us sisters out here," Kiwi said. She downed another portion of bourbon, chasing it with her lager.

"Well if you can fix diesel engines, then you'd fit right in here. About all we do is oil refining and exporting."

"It's funny, you know, diesel," Kiwi said, feeling the first wave of booze permeate into her brain. "Hundreds of years old, and still about the most efficient engine ever made."

The bartender nodded politely.

Kiwi looked around, spotting a small Christmas tree on a shelf behind the bar. It was welded together from scrap metal and was complete with lights and a star on top. "I love the tree. Merry Christmas, by the way," she said, holding up her beer.

"Hey, Merry Christmas." The bartender poured herself a small measure of lager, held it up in cheers, and downed it.

Kiwi realized she hadn't given Christmas any thought yet. She should probably get something for Gideon and Dax. "Hey, this lager," she said. "You have cans?"

"Of course."

"And how about the bourbon?"

"Yup, got plenty of bottles."

"Can I get, like, five cases of the lager and two cases of the bourbon sent to my ship?" Kiwi asked. She would keep most of it for herself, but some of it she could give to Gideon and Dax for Christmas.

"Of course!" the bartender said, excited at the big order. She queued it up on her touchpad. "And where are you docked?"

"Concourse A, port 17."

"A17. And your ship's name?" the bartender asked.

"The *Isle of Skye*," Kiwi said.

"Perfect, and here you are," the bartender said, presenting the touchpad.

Kiwi tapped her phone to the pad, not even bothering to look at the price.

"Oi, Rosevine, you drinking already?" a Scottish cadence said from behind.

Kiwi turned around to see Gideon approaching the bar. "It's mid-afternoon," she said. "What else would I be doing?"

"You could be getting your shopping done," Gideon replied.

"Hello?" Kiwi said. "Do you not see this bag of gear? It's bigger than I am."

"Everything's bigger than you are," Gideon said.

Kiwi downed the rest of her bourbon and lager. "I'll take another of both, and whatever he wants," she said to the bartender.

"I'll, erm, I'll have a pint of that lager, love," Gideon said.

"You see how he does that?" Kiwi said to the bartender. "See how he yells at me for drinking and then starts drinking himself?" The bartender laughed, knowing they were just ribbing each other.

"That's because I've seen how you drink," Gideon said. The bartender served up their drinks. "Thanks, love. Anyway, how do you like the station? It's flowing with diesel. Half the weapons at the gunsmith run on the stuff. You'd make a killing just working on engines here all day."

"Nah, I make more money with you, and it's more fun," Kiwi said. She held up her fresh lager and clinked glasses with Gideon. "Merry Christmas."

"Merry Christmas," Gideon said. "Speaking of, don't spoil your dinner. I just ordered a couple pot roasts for everyone."

"Pot roasts?" Kiwi asked. "They have beef here?"

"Yes, and loads of it," Gideon said. "I guess they raise cattle down on Titan in those huge bio-domes. And corn. I hope you like corn, because that's about the only vegetable they have."

"Of course I love corn," Kiwi said, holding up her whiskey. "I'm drinking some right now."

"Is that bourbon?" Gideon asked. "Lemme have a sip."

Kiwi gave her captain the glass.

Gideon coughed. "*Woo!* They put diesel in that, too?"

"What are you complaining about?" Kiwi asked. "You like whiskey almost as much as I do."

"I like whiskey," Gideon said. "Not engine degreaser."

"Well don't be too ungrateful. I got you a bottle of it for Christmas."

"Way to spoil the surprise," Gideon said. "Anyway, you get everything you need already?"

Kiwi nodded, swallowing more lager. "We're set on electrodes, wires, ignitors, all that. Argon tanks are getting refilled now, and got what I need to fix the reloader. And you *have* to see this cute little dress I got for myself." She started going through her bag.

"The bloody hell you need a dress for?"

"Because I found out this station has a nightclub, and I need to go dancing."

Gideon shook his head. "Just mind yourself. There's more guys on this station than girls."

"He's right, dear," the bartender chimed in. "A cute little thing like you, the guys will be all over you."

"Good," Kiwi said. "That means I won't have to buy my own drinks. Anyway, how about you? Get the toys you were looking for?"

"Yeah. Got this beautiful lever-action katana. Pretty genius design."

"Oh!" Kiwi exclaimed. "Yeah, I've seen those. That's the, uh, the Stetson-Whatever one, right? With the plasma cutting cartridges?"

Gideon nodded, not surprised by his technician's knowledge. "You'll like the revolver I got, too. A Remy-Larsson. Recoil would knock you clean over."

"Pfff," Kiwi scoffed. "I can handle recoil. It's this whiskey that's about to knock me over."

"You about finished up?" Gideon asked. "I'm gonna head back to the *Isle*."

"Yup!" Kiwi downed the last of her bourbon and chased it with the last of her lager. She paid her tab and slid off the barstool. "*Whoah!*"

"Whoah, you all right?" Gideon said, trying to catch her.

"I'm fine, I'm fine," she said, shrugging him off. She picked up the bag of gear and threw it over her shoulder. Her hair got caught in the straps again. "Goddammit," she said, pulling it out.

"Here let me get that," Gideon offered.

"No, no, I got it," Kiwi said. They started making their way through the industrial station, back to the ship. "Can we walk by the viewports? It's cool seeing the rings of Saturn so close."

"Of course."

"Oh, and I got a bunch of that beer and whiskey for everyone. Will go good with the pot roasts."

"That was nice of you," Gideon said. "Where they get that booze from, anyway?"

"They make it here," Kiwi said. She swayed and stumbled for a moment, but kept herself upright.

"Come on, lass," Gideon said. "You know, a tiny thing like you starts drinking early, then doesn't stop until she goes to bed, your brain can't rest, it can't dream. No wonder you never sleep well."

"Yeah, that's kinda the point," Kiwi said. "I don't like what my dreams show me."

3. Dax, The Engineer

Dax is forced to chaperone Kiwi's night out.

Dax threw a flurry of hooks, crosses. and jabs into the heavy bag from five meters away. He dialed the range down to three meters on his kinetic caestus, moved a couple meters closer, and repeated the punch combo.

Gideon and Kiwi walked in.

"You still working the bag?" Kiwi asked, a bundle of gear slung on her shoulder.

"Yeah, it's easy," Dax said. "You see, I think of you, and I can't stop punching the goddamn thing."

"That's his way of flirting with me," Kiwi said to Gideon.

"I'm attracted to women, Rosevine," Dax said. "Not little girls."

"I'm 25, jackass."

"Sure, kid."

"I see the Christmas spirit is alive and well in both of you," Gideon said. "Dax, I'm getting a nice spread sent over here, so don't spoil your dinner."

"And I got you some beer and whiskey for Christmas, Dax," Kiwi said, leaving the rec hall.

"Just get me a life-sized printout of yourself so I can paste it on this bag!" Dax shouted back. He turned to

Gideon. "Anyway, thanks for dinner. I got us a bunch of rib-eyes, by the way. Put 'em in the freezer."

"You knew this place had beef?" Gideon asked.

"Yeah, this station runs on beef, corn, and diesel," Dax said. "You didn't know that? I thought you'd been here before."

"Just once, and only because of that gun shop. That guy's got everything. Sure you don't need anything?"

Dax shook his head. "I'm set. I tuned up my kinetic fists earlier. They're working just fine, as you can see."

"By the way," Gideon said. "Kiwi's going out clubbing."

"Okay?" Dax said, shrugging his shoulders, wondering what that had to do with him.

"So, would you go with her? Make sure she doesn't get into too much trouble?"

Dax rolled his eyes. "I'm not her fucking chaperone, Gideon. Besides, going to a dance club is fucking torture."

"Well someone has to go with her, and you're the muscle, so make sure you tag along," Gideon said.

"I'm your engineer, not your muscle," Dax said.

"You're both. Besides, one look at you and just about anyone on this station will leave her alone."

"Hey!" Kiwi shouted, having returned. "What do you think? Isn't it cute?" She was wearing her new dress, a droopy Santa hat, and her work boots. Her rose vine tattoo was on full display. Somehow, the fashion all went together.

"You think anyone's gonna leave her alone looking like that?" Dax said to Gideon. "Half the goddamn station's gonna line up to buy her drinks."

"Yeah, that's the point!" Kiwi said.

"So why do they call you Kiwi?" a tipsy welder asked, dancing with no rhythm.

"Because my dad's from New Zealand, so he calls me his little kiwi," she said. She writhed away to the industrial music, keeping her drink in perfect balance. "Oh look, there he is! Hi dad!" she shouted at Dax, who rolled his eyes.

"Oh, your dad's *here*?" the welder said, sobering up quickly. He looked around, made eye contact with Dax, promptly stood upright, and said, "Hello, sir. Y-your daughter's a wonderful person," before escaping to the other end of the club.

Kiwi giggled. "You should've done a New Zealand accent," she said, still dancing. "That would've been hilarious."

"I don't do accents," Dax said in his East Texas cadence. "So what's the game? You just point at me when you're done with a guy?"

"Yeah! He was boring, anyway. I don't think he even got the joke. All these fucking welders are boring." She took a sip of her drink. "You wanna try this? It's a cocktail they call 'Rocket-Grade Kerosene', and holy shit it launches you into fucking orbit!"

Dax accepted the drink, downing the entire martini glass in one shot.

"Hey!" Kiwi exclaimed. "I said 'try' not 'down the whole thing'."

"That was your fourth goddamn drink," Dax said. "Besides, I needed something to take the edge off of having to watch your underage ass."

"Well now I need a fifth goddamn drink," Kiwi said. She slinked her way across the dance floor, catching the eye of someone who hadn't noticed Dax's towering frame. "Hey!" she shouted to her next victim. "You wouldn't want to buy me a drink, would you?"

"Can't buy you a drink if I don't know your name!" the young man said.

"Kiwi!" she shouted back, enjoying his banter.

The young man laughed. "Why do they call you Kiwi?"

"Because I have a tough skin," she said, shaking her hips, "but I'm super sweet to eat!"

"I can walk, you know," Kiwi said, cradled in Dax's massive arms.

"Your stumbling is slowing us up," Dax said. "You weigh next to nothing, and it's faster if I carry you."

"I wasn't even done dancing!"

"I was done watching you dance."

"And I was hoping to find a guy to split me in two," Kiwi said. "That last guy was pretty cute, and he even had a personality!"

Dax stayed quiet and focused on carrying his drunken technician back to the *Isle*.

"Why are you so, like, why do you hate fun?" Kiwi asked.

"I hate people," Dax said. "Not fun."

"But people are so much fun!"

"Especially when all your drinks are free," Dax said.

"Just put on a slinky dress like I do. It works every time!" Kiwi said. "Besides, I got us all whiskey and beer for Christmas, so I do actually pay for drinks sometimes. Did I tell you I got us whiskey and—?"

"Yes."

"Oh, that's right, I did," Kiwi said, just as they were coming up to port A17. Dax put her down. "And thank you for the ride, good sir. I will leave a positive review with your manager."

"You know what he got us for dinner, by the way?" Dax asked as they went through the airlock.

"Yeah, pot roasts, corn, and uh, more corn," Kiwi said.

"Pot roasts and corn, huh?" Dax said, looking at the spread.

"And beer!" Kiwi said, popping open a can of lager.

"And beer," Gideon echoed. "Where's Philly Phil?"

"Who knows, I'm hun-gray!" Kiwi said. She started carving herself some meat. "Oh shit, is that corn grilled? That's so cool!"

"Can we at least have a proper cheers before we dig in?" Gideon asked.

"We can't have nice things with her around," Dax said. "Christ, I can't even get a quiet evening to myself."

Kiwi belched, then said, "No no, he's right." She reached for the case of whiskey on the floor and produced a bottle. She poured a shot for Dax and Gideon. "What are we, uh, what are we cheers-ing? Us being space pirates?"

"We're more mercenaries than pirates," Gideon said. "But why not. Merry Christmas, and to us being space pirates."

Dax held up his whiskey. "*'Yo ho ho'.*"

"*'And a bottle of rum'*," Kiwi said, taking a pull of whiskey straight from the bottle.

4. Philly Cheesesteak, The 4th Crewman

Philly Phil takes a couple of naps and gets some pot roast.

Philly Cheesesteak woke up in a vent near the reactor. He yawned, took a long, luxurious stretch, and shook his head awake. He could hear Dax working on something there in engineering, and ventured out to say hi.

"Oh hey," Dax said. "I thought you might be down here."

Philly walked up and bumped his head into Dax's leg. Dax crouched down and gave him some scratches.

"You just wake up?" Dax asked.

Philly blinked his eyes.

"Nice, warm reactor. That's why engineering's your favorite spot to sleep, huh?"

Philly bumped his head into Dax again.

"I got us a bunch of beef, by the way. I'll give you some whenever we have it."

Philly sat down and looked up at Dax, his eyes wide.

"I don't have any for you now," Dax said. "It's all in the freezer."

Philly looked down and away. He licked his mouth.

"Well look, I'm trying to catch up on some stuff here. Kiwi's going out dancing in a bit and apparently I gotta be her fucking chaperone. I think she's hanging out in the armory. You should go bug her."

"*Br-r-r-r-eh,*" Philly said before standing up and strolling off.

The crew kept the doors closed for the most part, so Philly had learned to navigate the ventilation system to get from room to room. He was coming up to the armory, and whatever industrial rock Kiwi was blasting was making an absolute cacophony in the vents. He tried pivoting his ears in different directions to lessen the sound, but it didn't help.

When he emerged from the vent, he saw Kiwi was huddled over on a workbench.

"*Myeh,*" he greeted, but Kiwi couldn't hear him over the music. He came up right beside her and repeated himself. "*Myeh!*" but Kiwi still couldn't hear him. He knew she didn't like it when he jumped up on the workbench, so he gently tapped her leg.

Kiwi looked down. "Oh hey little Philly Cheesesteak!" She turned the music way down. "Where'd you come from?"

Philly decided to jump up on the bench anyway.

"No, you asshole! That's dangerous!" Kiwi scolded. She picked him up, and he put his paws on her shoulder. "Ohhhh," she said. "You just wanted me to hold you?"

Philly purred.

"Well these are my work clothes, so go ahead and dig in with those claws. I got a new dress today, by the way. I'd show you, but I gotta finish up here and then shower before I head out."

"*Mao?*" Philly asked.

"Oh this? It's my whip, see?" She moved to an angle so he could see the work bench. "It's really cool. It's got a tungsten tip that strikes a plasma arc when it hits. I was just soldering some of the electronics in the handle. How about you? You just wake up?"

Philly blinked slowly.

"Well here, I'm gonna put you down, okay? Christ, you weigh more than I do."

"*M-r-r-r-r-eh.*"

"Yeah yeah, I know, everything weighs more than I do," Kiwi said. She put him down, then went to the entrance and opened the door. "Look, I'm gonna finish up, then I gotta go shower cuz I'm goin' out dan-sing! Go bug Dax or Gideon."

Philly sat for a moment. He thought about staying, but Kiwi was going to blast that music again. He stood up and walked towards a different air vent.

It didn't take long for Philly to find Gideon. He was usually somewhere in the front of the ship. This time he was on the bridge, talking to a client over videochat.

"Oh no, we can do it," Gideon said. "I'm just not sure why you need a group like us. Wouldn't it be better to just find someone inside the company?"

"*Usually yes, but these guys are up to some shady shit,*" the client said.

"They're a pharmaceutical company," Gideon said. "Of course they're up to shady shit."

Philly slinked up to Gideon unnoticed.

"*I mean, you're not wrong, but apparently what they're doing out there is as illegal as it gets. They've got a small team of armed guards, probably all ex-military, at that facility.*"

Philly jumped into Gideon's lap.

"Dah shit!" Gideon exclaimed.

"*You all right?*"

"Yeah," Gideon said. "Sorry, the fucking cat just startled me." He stroked Philly.

"You have a cat on your ship?"

"Yeah, they keep the rats out."

Philly purred and bumped his head into Gideon's beard.

"Oh, didn't know rats were a problem in space."

"Yeah, but they're not a problem when one of your crew is a cat."

"What's the cat's name?"

"Philly Cheesesteak."

The client laughed. *"How he end up with that name?"*

"It's a long story," Gideon said, not wanting to go into the details. "Anyway, you were saying?"

"Yeah, so the facility is small and it's a secret even to most of the company. I think they set it up as a subsidiary with a different name."

Gideon nodded, still petting Philly. "Sounds like whatever they're doing is so illegal that they won't report anything even if they get robbed."

"Exactly. Now, we're mostly just looking for information. We have an idea of what they're doing, but we want evidence."

"What *are* they doing?"

"I'm keeping that in the dark until I know you're gonna take the job."

Gideon narrowed his eyes. Philly flicked his tail. "I like to know what I'm getting paid to do before I do it," Gideon said.

"I know, but this is at the request of the person who paid me to find someone."

"Lemme guess," Gideon said. "A rival pharmaceutical company."

The client smirked. *"Will neither confirm nor deny."*

"Well let me run it by the crew. When you need an answer?"

"Tomorrow work for you?"

"Tomorrow's Christmas, but sure. Will let you know."

"Merry Christmas."

"Same to you." Gideon closed the call. "What're you doing sneaking up on me when I'm with a client?"

Philly blinked his eyes.

"What did you think of him?" Gideon asked.

Philly flicked his tail again.

"Yeah, I didn't like it, either," Gideon said. "But I've worked with him before, and we do shady things all the time."

Philly looked up at Gideon.

"Well what would you have me do? We have to make money, and if I tell him no, I'm probably losing future business with him. Besides, pharmaceuticals pays a lot."

Philly closed his eyes and rested his head on Gideon.

"By the way, I got us some pot roasts for tonight. Stop by the mess hall when we're there. I'll give you a few bites."

Philly started purring again.

"Look, you're not gonna like this, but I've got to get up." Gideon picked him up.

"Meh-r-r-r-r-eh," Philly protested.

"I know, I know," Gideon said. "But I've got more captain things to do. Go hunt some rats, or something."

Philly woke up from another nap. He was on Kiwi's bed, having found her in the shower earlier and followed her back to her room where she got changed. He yawned, stretched, and jumped into the vent.

He was hungry, and winded through the vents on his way to the mess hall. He could hear Gideon, Kiwi, and

Dax's voices as he approached. He heard Kiwi belch just as he jumped out of the vent and into the mess hall.

"We're more mercenaries than pirates," Gideon said. "But why not. Merry Christmas, and to us being space pirates."

Dax held up his whiskey. "*'Yo ho ho'.*"

"*'And a bottle of rum',*" Kiwi said, taking a pull of whiskey straight from the bottle.

Philly strutted up to the table, tail held high.

"Oh look!" Kiwi said. "It's Philly Phil the Cheesesteak!"

"Oh, hey there," Dax said, holding out a hand. Philly rubbed his cheek on it.

"Oi, you little shit," Gideon said. "Come on up."

Philly found a good launch angle, then leapt up to the table. He went straight for the pot roast, whiskers flared, sniffing intently.

"Hey, that's not for cats, you little asshole!" Kiwi said.

"No, no, it's all right," Gideon said, carving a few slivers of meat from the roast. "I told him earlier he could have some."

"Can cats eat pot roast?" Dax asked.

"Apparently this one can," Gideon said. Philly lapped up the slivers from his hand, then looked at him wide-eyed, demanding more. "Just a little bit more, all right?"

"Hey, Philly Phil," Kiwi said, giving him a pet. "You can sleep with me tonight, because uncle Dax scared away all the guys at the club."

"Just following the captain's orders," Dax said.

"The fuck, Gideon?" Kiwi said.

"Oh don't start, Rosevine," Gideon said, letting Philly lick the meat juices from his hand. "Last time we docked, you go missing for two days, only for me to find out you're fucking the captain of the *Philadelphia*, who is a good friend of mine, by the way, and who has about 20 years on you."

Kiwi shrugged her shoulders. "I have daddy issues."

"You're a woman," Dax said. "You all have daddy issues."

"Oh shut up, Dax," Kiwi said. "Besides, you love Philly Phil the most. And that captain of the *Philadelphia*, what was his name?"

"Thomas," Gideon said.

"Yes, Thomas! My god, he was such a gentleman. Anyway, he gets a little pussy, and we get a little pussy cat, it's a fair trade!"

Dax and Gideon just rolled their eyes.

"Oh!" Kiwi exclaimed. "You know what we should do? We should totally do Philly cheesesteaks for real, like get the bread, get the cheese, and there's a ton of beef here already, you know?"

Dax and Gideon made eye contact and nodded. Kiwi had a good point.

"Mreow!" Philly said, impatient for more pot roast.

5. An Easter Egg Hunt in Space

Gideon takes the crew to a moon around Uranus, Kiwi makes a sex joke, and Dax gets a carton of eggs.

Kiwi writhed to her industrial rock while spot welding a titanium filament to her power whip, just as Dax walked into the armory.

"Kiwi," Dax said.

But Kiwi didn't hear a thing, and kept jamming to her music and spot welding away.

"Kiwi!" Dax shouted.

But still, she couldn't hear him, and kept up her ballet of welding and dancing.

"KIWI!" Dax screamed.

Kiwi perked up and looked towards the door. "Oh hey, Dax!" she shouted over the music.

"Shut the fucking music off!" he shouted back.

Kiwi rolled her eyes. "Fine!" She keyed her phone's interface and shut down the reverberating rock.

"The hell are you doing?" Dax asked. "Some new, stupid invention?"

"Yeah, it's a new invention," Kiwi said with sarcasm. "Get this. It's a dick that you can suck."

Dax didn't bat an eye. "Well fellate it to completion soon. Gideon wants to see us both on the bridge."

"Why are *you* telling me this?" Kiwi asked. "Why didn't he just message me?"

"He *did* message you," Dax said. "You were too busy blasting the armory with that industrial shit to notice."

Kiwi queued up her phone, finally noticing the message from Gideon. "Oh yeah! You're right!"

Dax rolled his eyes and headed for the bridge.

"Fucking eggs?" Kiwi asked in disbelief.

"Yes," Gideon confirmed in his Scottish cadence. "Fucking eggs."

"Our job is seriously just to collect a bunch of eggs?" Dax asked.

"Look," Gideon said. "I don't know the finer points of pharmaceutical development, all I know is our current employers want a crate of eggs from this place. Apparently they're used all the time in biological weapons, vaccine development, or something, and we've been hired to secure some."

"I mean, it *is* Easter," Kiwi pointed out. "May as well go on an egg hunt, am I right, boys?"

Dax rolled his eyes.

Gideon got back to the point. "We're coming into orbit around Umbriel in a few hours. Soon as we do, we're dropping."

"It would've been nice to know this sooner, Gideon," Kiwi complained.

"I did let you know sooner," Gideon said. "You just couldn't be bothered to see my message."

"So what do we need to do between now and then?" Dax asked.

"Well, a place this far out, yeah they got security, but they're bored to tears because nothing ever happens out here. Ready up your usual arsenal, and make sure you're wearing your pressure suits, and rig your face-scrambling software for all the cameras they'll have."

Philly Cheesesteak sauntered onto the bridge from an air vent.

"Oh, hey, Philly Phil!" Kiwi said.

Philly Cheesesteak walked up to Kiwi and bashed his head into her leg. She scratched his face and he purred loudly.

"So," Gideon said. "If you're paying attention, Kiwi, go suit up, get your shit in order, and make sure you're ready to drop in," he checked his phone, "two hours and 47-minutes."

"They seriously don't even know we're coming?" Kiwi asked, still scratching Philly Cheesesteak.

"Detecting a ship you don't know is approaching you is like trying to spot a mosquito from the fucking moon," Dax said. "Or maybe they didn't teach you that on your Wisconsin farm."

"Says the East Texas hick," Kiwi said back.

"Two hours, 45-minutes," Gideon said. "We're dropping then."

"Dax, you in position?" Gideon asked over encrypted shortwave.

"Of course I am," Dax answered. *"Got one bored security asshole down this corridor. Can knock him out from ten meters with my kinetic fists. Just give the word."*

"Kiwi, how about you? You in position?" Gideon asked.

"I mean, I'm doing doggy-style through this vent at the moment, if that's what you mean," she answered.

Gideon rolled his eyes. "Are you in fucking *position?"*

"It's fucking dark in here, Gideon!" Kiwi protested. *"Gimme another minute, or five."*

Gideon exhaled sharply. "Okay," he said. "Dax, I may need you to—"

"Nevermind, I'm in place!" Kiwi squealed over the shortwave.

Gideon reevaluated. "Okay, um, tell me what you see."

"Got one asshole with a slung net taser walking away from me," Kiwi said. *"And another asshole with a cigar and bad forearm tattoos walking towards me."*

"Yeah," Dax confirmed. *"Forearm tattoo asshole with the cigar is the one walking away from me."*

"Okay," Gideon said. "Dax, I'm gonna cut the power. Slip out and head to your right as soon as I do. Kiwi, hang tight for a moment."

"Cool, Gideon," Kiwi said. *"I can do doggy-style all day."*

Gideon flipped the safety off of his lever-action katana, and cut the power node next to him. Lights went out, as did the power to the door they were looking to get into. Lazy security this far out in the solar system hadn't planned for backups.

Dax, in spite of his massive frame, slipped out of his hiding spot stealthily, and through the now-open door.

"Dax," Gideon, said into his radio. "The package all set?"

"Yeah, Gideon," Dax said sarcastically. *"The fucking cardboard egg crate I'm putting the eggs in is all set. How many of these things you need, by the way?"*

"As many as you can fit," Gideon responded.

"Hey, Gideon," Kiwi said over the shortwave. *"Those guards are going apeshit now that the power is out. Need me to distract them?"*

"Yes!" Gideon said in panic. "Dax, you about done?"

"Crate filled, heading back out to the dropship."

"Great, meet you there."

"You seriously just needed a dozen eggs in a fucking cardboard crate?" Dax asked, strapping himself into place, getting ready to launch back to the *Isle of Skye*.

"Like I told you." Gideon said. "I don't know how these pharmaceuticals replicate their viral shit, but apparently it's all about the eggs."

"Whatever you say, boss," Dax said. giving a mock salute.

Gideon was about to strap himself in, when his jaw dropped 10-feet. "Oh shit," he said.

"What?" Dax asked.

"Where the fuck is Kiwi?"

"Normally I don't do threesomes," Kiwi said, stretching herself out luxuriously, power whip in hand.

The security guard with the cigar tossed it onto the walkway and cracked his knuckles.

The security guard with the net taser racked it like a shotgun.

"But for you two," Kiwi said, unfurling her whip and switching the power on, "I'll make an exception."

6. Kiwi's Threesome

Gideon loses his temper at Kiwi, Dax loses his temper at Gideon, and Kiwi gets kidnapped.

"Normally I don't do threesomes," Kiwi said, stretching herself out luxuriously, power whip in hand.

The security guard with the cigar tossed it onto the walkway and cracked his knuckles.

The security guard with the net taser racked it like a shotgun.

"But for you two," Kiwi said, unfurling her whip and switching the power on, "I'll make an exception."

They moved towards her at perpendicular angles. Net Taser slowly raised his weapon. Cigar got ready to lunge.

Kiwi was just about to crack her whip when Net Taser suddenly crumpled to his right, as though he had taken a shot to his kidney. Then he crumpled to his left. Then his jaw lurched to his right, and he fell to the steel-grate floor, knocked out.

Cigar took advantage of Kiwi's momentary confusion and lunged for her.

But Kiwi gave a disinterested flick of her whip, lacerating his face, while the whip's power surge knocked him out. She made her way to Net Taser to find out just what the hell had happened to him, only to see Dax emerge with his kinetic fists. He had delivered a nasty combo to Net Taser from 10 meters away.

"Jesus Christ, Dax," she said. "Every time I try to have a little fun, you ruin it!"

"You're fuckin welcome!" Dax said. "Get your ass over here, we gotta get to the drop ship now!"

Kiwi rolled her eyes and followed Dax.

"Faster!" he shouted.

Kiwi started jogging.

"You wanna tell me what in the fuck you were doing back there!" Gideon chided as the dropship made its rough liftoff. He winced, feeling the compression in his spine.

"I did what you fucking told me, Gideon!" Kiwi shouted back. "I asked you! 'Hey, Gideon, need me to distract these fucking guards?' And you say, 'Yes, do it, now!' So I did *exactly* what you told me, like a good little girl, and somehow it's *my* fault?"

"By 'distraction' I meant making some kind of noise in the goddamn vent!"

"Well you didn't exactly communicate that to me, now did you!"

Dax, desperate to stop the screaming, actually came to Kiwi's defense. "Gideon, she distracted them, we got away."

"Yes!" Gideon conceded. "And both of those guards are still alive and waking up right about now, and can give a full description of you, Kiwi! Jesus Christ, do you need me to tell you how to wipe your arse, too?"

Kiwi, mouth trembling, and on the verge of crying, found a corner of the dropship to fixate on.

"Cool it, man," Dax said, irritated at his captain's blame game. "Not her fault you weren't explicit enough."

"Well that's a first," Gideon chided. "Never thought I'd ever see you defend her."

"Hey!" Dax, shouted. "I'm the one that grabbed those stupid, fucking eggs, not you. I'm the one who held my cool, not you. I'm the one who ran back for her, *not you!*"

For the first time, Gideon outright wanted to punch Dax. But he knew he was right, and stayed silent, looking out the viewport. They all simmered silently for the rest of the ride back to the *Isle.*

When they docked, Gideon was the first one out. "I'll be on the bridge," he said, curtly. "I'll spin us up for a slingshot out of here. Both of you get to engineering."

Dax and Kiwi took their time unstrapping themselves. "Thanks, Dax," Kiwi mumbled, head hung low.

"Don't worry, half-pint," he said. He grabbed the insulated case that carried the carton of eggs. "He messed up, not you, and he knows it." He was about to head to the mess hall to put the eggs in cold storage, but Kiwi's posture was still slumped and depressed.

"By the way," he added. "Nice crack of that whip back there."

Kiwi tried to suppress a proud smirk. "I *told* you it works."

They left the drop ship and boarded the *Isle*. Philly Cheesesteak greeted them, tail high. "*Br-r-r-r-eh?*" he asked.

"Hey, Philly Phil," Kiwi answered. "Just getting back from a job. Uncle Gideon's grumpy, so stay off the bridge for now."

"*Mr-r-r-eh,*" Philly Cheesesteak acknowledged.

"Meet me in engineering after you drop your gear off," Dax said.

Kiwi gave a casual salute.

"*Mr-r-raow?*" Philly asked.

"Yeah, you can come, too," Dax said to Philly. "But I gotta stop at the mess hall first. Come with me. I'll grab you a snack."

Gideon waited until they were leaving Uranus space and on autopilot back to Titan before he went looking for Kiwi. He tapped his phone.

"Hey," Kiwi answered.

"Hey, Rosevine," Gideon said. "Where are you? I owe you an apology."

"Just hanging out in the mess."

"Hang out a little longer. I'll be down in a sec."

Gideon made his way to the mess hall. He saw Kiwi casually browsing her phone, a plate of half-eaten food in front of her, along with an open can of beer.

"Christ, you drinking already?" Gideon asked, sitting down.

Kiwi rolled her eyes and didn't even look at Gideon. "You come here to apologize or criticize?"

"All right," Gideon said, holding up his hands. "You're right, I'm sorry. I didn't give you clear instructions. I got a lot riding on this gig, but that's no excuse. I'm sorry."

Kiwi glanced up from her phone to finally look at Gideon. She grabbed her beer can and raised it. "Apology accepted," she said, before taking a swig.

Gideon held up a fist in a mock cheers. Then he laid on the bad news.

"All right, look," he said, thinking about how he was going to deliver this. "We get to Titan station in about a week."

"Yeah," Kiwi said. "Can't wait to stretch my legs a bit."

Gideon let loose a sigh. "Yeah, but here's the thing. I'm gonna need you to stay on the *Isle* while we're docked."

Kiwi snapped her neck away from her phone and glared at Gideon.

"Look," Gideon said. "You didn't fuck up, I did. But the fact stands that those guards saw you. Face-scrambling software aside, they *saw* you. Which means they can describe you, and with Titan being the closest station, even all the way out here, you can bet they'll have people looking for you there."

Kiwi sighed, but knew Gideon was right.

"So listen," Gideon said. "As soon as we dock, I'm delivering the package, and we'll get our payout soon."

Kiwi huffed. "I still can't believe we came all the way out here for a carton of fucking eggs."

"Don't worry, Rosevine," Gideon said, standing up. "You'll believe it well enough when you see what the payout is."

Kiwi took another swig of beer. "Sorry, Gideon."

"It's all right, love," Gideon said.

"I don't know," Kiwi said, looking in the mirror and talking to Philly Cheesesteak. "Should I go goth girl, or pink little cupcake?"

Philly flicked his tail in protest.

"I feel like the whole diesel, industrial thing at that place, I should do goth."

Philly flicked his tail again.

"Well you're no help," Kiwi said.

Philly stood up, then pointed himself away from Kiwi.

"Like, I went goth last time, and lots of guys hit on me then," Kiwi said.

Philly flicked his tail twice, emphasizing his irritation.

"Fine, Philly Phil," Kiwi said. "Don't care. I'm going out."

"Mr-r-raow!" Philly said.

"Oh, come on!" Kiwi said back. "No one knows who I am. Besides, I haven't gotten laid in god-knows how many months. We're docking, I'm going out, I don't care what Gideon says."

Philly snorted, flicking his tail a few more times.

"Goth girl it is," Kiwi said.

Gideon secured the eggs in a cold storage suitcase. "This it?" he asked.

"What do you mean?" Dax asked. "You know that's what we got."

Gideon sighed, then said, "I know, I'm sorry. It's just, you have no idea how much these are worth."

"I'll have a good idea once I see the payout," Dax said.

"Oh trust me," Gideon said. "That you will."

Kiwi writhed to the industrial beats, martini glass in hand, enjoying the strobe lights in the dance club. So far, she'd blown off every guy who'd come up to her.

But then she caught the eye of an attractive guy at the bar. He had a different demeanor than the techs, welders, and station regulars. He looked like a professional of some type in his 30s, and had a confident stance.

She slinked up to him.

"Hey," she shouted over the music.

"Hey," the man said back, not even looking at her.

Kiwi was too intrigued to stop. "You know, usually I'm the one who plays hard to get!"

"I could tell," the man responded, still looking at his phone. "Every guy that's come up to you, you've sent them retreating with their tails between their legs."

"You noticed!" Kiwi squealed. "Well don't worry, you're safe. You haven't approached me at all. In fact, you're not even paying attention to me!

The guy finally cracked a smile and looked at Kiwi. "Sorry," he said. "Bit an introvert. I'm Jason."

"Uh oh," Kiwi said, shaking his hand.

"What?" he asked.

"You're in big trouble, Jason," she said. She leaned into his ear. "Introverts are my favorite type of guy to ruin." She downed the rest of her drink.

Jason laughed again. "Can I get you another one of those?"

Having delivered the eggs to his contact and accepted payment, Gideon strolled back onto the *Isle*. He breathed a sigh of relief. He hadn't realized how stressed he'd been carrying a case with contents worth more than any contract he'd ever fulfilled.

He called up Dax. "Hey, where are you?"

"Mess."

Gideon made his way to the mess hall to find Dax sipping some coffee. Philly Cheesesteak was on the table, whiskers flared, trying to get his attention. When he saw Gideon enter the mess, he looked at him and said, *"Mreh!"* impatiently.

"Well, good morning to you, too," Gideon responded. He sat down at the table. "You not feed him yet?"

"Oh no, I did," Dax said. "Little fucker's been bugging me all night and all morning. Can't tell what the hell he wants."

Philly huffed and flicked his tail.

"Kiwi not up yet?" Gideon asked.

"Myah!" Philly said, trying to make a point.

"Don't know," Dax said. He sipped his coffee. "Don't care."

"Meh, br-r-r-reh," Philly said, jumping off the table, taking a few steps, and then looking back to see if Gideon and Dax were going to follow him.

"What the hell's with you today?" Gideon asked.

Philly took a few more steps, then looked back to see if Gideon or Dax got the point.

Gideon's jaw dropped in realization. "Oh shit," he said, pulling out his phone. He didn't bother calling Kiwi, he just checked if her phone was anywhere on the ship. Sure enough, it wasn't.

"What?" Dax asked.

"Where the fuck is Kiwi?"

Kiwi snorted awake. She was in a chair, her face and arms on a table, her mouth was painfully dry, and her lips slimy. She managed to open her eyes enough to see a clean, sterile room. She had no idea where she was or how she got there, she just knew she wasn't on the station.

The door opened, and someone came in. An even bigger someone was right behind him.

Kiwi tried to prop up her head and see who it was. "Oh, yeah," she said through squinted eyes. "You, you were, uh, you're Jameson?"

"No."

"Jackson?"

"No."

Kiwi snapped her finger. "Justin!"

"Jason."

"Right! Jason!" Kiwi exclaimed. "Anyway, Jason, I'm sure we had a great time last night, but do you have, like, a gallon of water? Cuz this girl is thirsty. And hungover. And probably still drunk."

The larger someone behind Jason muttered a few things to him privately. Jason appeared to ignore it. He sat down, opposite Kiwi.

"Here's what's gonna happen, dear," Jason said, placing a jet injector on the table. "We know you were involved in a little thievery recently, and you're going to tell us everything you know, everyone you work with, and you're gonna cooperate nicely."

7. Detective Philly Cheesesteak

Philly Cheesesteak gets aboard the station, Gideon and Dax follow him, and Kiwi has a bad hangover.

"Here's what's gonna happen, dear," Jason said, placing a jet injector on the table. "We know you were involved in a little thievery recently, and you're going to tell us everything you know, everyone you work with, and you're gonna cooperate nicely."

Kiwi, eyes still not quite open, said, "Justin, I'll tell you anything you want for a gallon of ice water right now."

"It's Jason."

"Right, anyway, Jason, do you even know what a hangover is?"

Jason scoffed, unable to get a read on Kiwi.

Kiwi painfully opened her eyes, noticing the larger man in the room. "How about you, big guy? You ever have plate steel forge-welded to your fucking skull? Because that's what I'm going through right now. Jesus Christ, did you guys slip me something? Because I didn't drink that much."

"Hey!" Jason shouted.

Kiwi squinted again, holding her head. "Christ, keep your voice down."

"Are you even listening to me sweetheart? Do you know what's about to happen here?" he asked, pointing at the jet injector.

Kiwi finally noticed the injector. "Please tell me that's a shot of electrolytes."

"No, dear," Jason said. "It's a shot of Truthinol."

"*PFffffffff!!*" Kiwi blurted out. "No," she said, laughing uncontrollably.

Jason didn't know how to respond.

Kiwi kept laughing. "*'Truthinol',*" she mocked, still laughing. "How many billions does a pharmaceutical company spend on marketing, and the best name they come up with is fucking *Truth*inol?"

Jason was getting irritated. The larger man tried to say something to him while Kiwi was busy with her hysterics, but Jason waved him off. "Hey!" he shouted again.

Kiwi calmed down, but was still giggling. "Lemme guess. You inject me with that and I'll tell you the truth, right?" she asked.

Jason leaned forward. "I inject you with this, and you'll be telling me every dark, dirty little secret you've ever had."

Kiwi feigned a giggle, and then in a flash she snatched the injector, held it to her own neck, and pulled the trigger.

Jason and the larger man were both stunned.

Kiwi smiled, then her eyes rolled to the back of her head, and she slunk in her chair. "You guys were fucking dumb not to retrain me," she said.

The larger man went to Jason and said, "I told you, you can't inject her with that shit if she's dehydrated or still drun—"

"Shut up!" Jason said.

"You know, guys, *whoah,*" Kiwi said, losing her balance, even in her chair. "We didn't have to do this. I told you, a gallon of water and I would've told you anything. Hell, you could've let big guy here throw me around the room and have his way with me, and I would've told you anything."

"Why the hell didn't you restrain her!" the larger man asked Jason.

"Shut up!" Jason said again.

"So," Kiwi said, slumping back in the chair with a raised eyebrow. "Ask me anything."

"We've gotta get her on IV fluids fast, or she's gonna lose it," the larger man warned.

But Jason was too keen to interrogate her. "Why's your name Kiwi?"

"Because my hair is so thick, and I was so cute as a kid, and I waddled around like a tiny bird, so my dad called me his little Kiwi."

Jason scoffed, not believing her, and not believing the Truthinol hadn't kicked in yet.

"You don't even get the joke, do you?" Kiwi said.

"Who do you work for?" Jason asked.

"I work for King Kiwi of New Zealand. You see, he trained me from a young age to have this Wisconsin accent so no one would suspect me." Kiwi pointed at the jet injector. "This stuff doesn't work, does it?"

Jason turned around to the larger man, who scolded him. "I told you! If she's still drunk, that stuff doesn't bind to her brain like it's supposed to! It's just gonna dehydrate her more and wreck her kidneys! We need to get her on IV fluids now before—"

"Oh fuck me, I don't feel good," Kiwi said on queue, before throwing up on the table and into her own hair. Her head and arms squirmed in her own vomit, unable to lift herself up from the table.

"Oh Jesus," Jason exclaimed.

"You gonna listen to me or not!" the larger gentleman shouted.

"You think we have IV fluids on this fucking ship?" Jason shouted back.

The larger man loosed a frustrated sigh. He went to pick up Kiwi.

"What are you doing!" Jason demanded.

"Either we get her to the station infirmary, or she dies here and we learn nothing."

"What are we gonna tell them? You can't just drop off a girl in that shape!"

"Sure we can," the larger man said. He hefted Kiwi's small frame and started carrying her out. "'What's wrong with her,' they'll ask, and we tell them, 'don't know, just found her outside the nightclub, she's clearly wasted,' and we leave it at that."

"Philly, knock that shit off now!" Gideon shouted at the cat, but Philly Cheesesteak hissed, insisting that he come with them.

"Look, stop fighting him," Dax said as they opened the airlock to the station. "He's made up his mind, and you're just pissing him off now."

The three of them made their way onto the station, Philly trotting in the lead.

"He's gonna get lost," Gideon said.

"He's not gonna get lost. He knows where we're docked, and he's microchipped. He'll be fine."

Philly led the way down the corridor. At the docking ring intersection, he stopped for a moment, sniffed the air, then trotted to the right.

Gideon was on his phone, still trying to find Kiwi. "She's still not answering," he said.

Dax followed Philly. "This way," he said.

"Why this way?" Gideon asked, distracted.

"Just trust me."

Dax kept leading the way, but was actually following Philly Cheesesteak. He quickly realized where they were headed as they entered the habitat ring. "She's probably been to the night club," he said.

"How do you know that?" Gideon asked.

"Where the hell else you think she'd go on this station?"

Philly Cheesesteak arrived at the entrance, but the nightclub was closed. He looked up at Dax, then looked at the club, then looked back at Dax and said, *"Mr-r-r-r-r-ah!"*

"They're closed, asshole," Dax said.

"Meh-r-r-r-ryah," Philly said back.

Dax sighed. "Fine," he said. He turned to Gideon. "You get anything on your phone yet?"

"Actually, yeah," Gideon said. "Looks like she's on the other side of the ring. Jesus, maybe in the infirmary."

"Myah-b-r-r-r-reh!" Philly said, tapping Gideon's leg and trotting off in the direction of the infirmary.

"Well go see if she's there. I'm gonna check this place out."

Gideon and Philly Cheesesteak entered the infirmary and went to the reception desk. "Hey, love," Gideon said.

"Hi, can I help you?" the receptionist said.

Philly mumbled, then trotted off towards the patient area.

"Yeah, I'm looking for a young woman, weighs all of 90 pounds, most of that's her hair, has a large rosevine tattoo across her body?"

Philly looked back at Gideon. *"Br-r-r-ryah!"*

"Oh yeah," the receptionist said, pulling up a chart. "We didn't get a name on her. A couple of guys dropped her off not too long ago. Do you know her?"

"Yeah, she's one of my crewman," Gideon said. "Her name's Kiwi."

"Meh-r-r-reh," Philly said impatiently, before trotting back into the patient area.

"Oh, that would explain why she kept saying 'Kiwi.'"

"All right if I see her?" Gideon asked.

"Of course, here, let me take you back to her." The receptionist led the way back. "She's mostly stable now, just a case of alcohol poisoning. We've got her hooked up to some IVs, but she'll be fine before long." When they came to Kiwi's bed, Philly Cheesesteak was already perched on it, licking her face, rousing her awake.

Kiwi woke up, irritated at the cat tongue on her cheek. When she opened her eyes and saw the cat, she said, "Ohh, Philly Phil, where'd you come from?"

"Hey, Rosevine, how are ya?" Gideon asked.

When Kiwi noticed Gideon, she said, "Oh fuck, how much trouble am I in now?"

"None. You all right? What happened?"

"I was," Kiwi said, seeming to drift in and out of consciousness. "Kidnapped. Got drugged. Was on a ship. I don't," she trailed off. Philly Cheesesteak licked her face until she snapped awake again.

"You got kidnapped? What happened?"

Kiwi shook her head. "Don't know. Was in the club. Met some hot fucker named Jason. Woke up on a ship. It's gotta be stationed here."

"What did they want?"

"Wanted to," Kiwi drifted off again. Philly licked her face again. "Wanted to know who I worked for. Don't worry. Didn't tell them a thing. Tried to drug me, but didn't work."

"What else do you know about them?" Gideon asked.

"I," Kiwi said, drowsy. "I really need to sleep, Gideon."

He patted her head as she passed out for good. "Don't worry, kid. I'm not going anywhere." He knew he had to stay put in case whoever dropped her off would be back. He checked his phone and called Dax.

"Hey," Dax answered.

"Hey, mate, you find anything?"

"Actually I did. Looks like some jackass picked her up from the club. Bartender told me about it. Have an idea where they might be docked."

Philly Cheesesteak was listening intently.

"Kiwi's saying it was some hot bloke named Jason. I'm gonna stick by her bed in the infirmary, make sure whoever dropped her off doesn't come back looking for her. She says they were trying to interrogate her, tried to drug her, but it went all wrong."

Philly Cheesesteak had heard enough. He jumped off the bed and galloped towards the exit.

"Oi, where you going!" Gideon demanded.

Philly Cheesesteak retraced his steps back to the nightclub, where he knew he would find Dax's scent. A number of people on the station tried to approach him, thinking they'd found a stray, but Philly ignored them and trotted along, following Dax's scent away from the club.

He was lucky Dax hadn't showered yet today. His scent was easy to follow.

He eventually found the stairwell Dax had taken down to docking ring C, just one level below the habitat ring. He trotted along the ring, following his crewmate's scent, until he found Dax casually leaning against a viewing port near a docked ship.

"Meow-r-r-ryah!" he greeted, tail held high.

"Hey, little Cheesesteak," Dax greeted, kneeling down and scratching his head. "How the hell you find me down here?"

Philly purred.

Dax stood up. "I talked to one of the bartenders at the nightclub. I think this is where they first took Kiwi. Just been hanging out, see if anyone comes or goes."

Philly tasted the air. He caught a vague fragrance of someone he'd smelled on Kiwi. He walked a few paces to the corridor leading to the nearest parked ship. Whoever had taken Kiwi to the infirmary had come from there. He stared down the airlock.

"What?" Dax said. "See something you like?"

Philly looked at Dax, then looked back down the corridor, just as the airlock to the ship opened. Philly shifted.

Dax looked back at his phone.

Philly watched the figure coming down the corridor towards the ring. He looked away, so as not to appear aggressive, and instead tasted the air as the figure walked by.

Philly had his mark.

He walked up to Dax as the figure walked by, and hissed. *"Hhhhhhhheh!"*

Dax looked up, immediately finding who Philly was hissing at. "Are you serious?" he asked.

Philly hissed again. The figure kept walking, oblivious to Philly and Dax.

But Dax sized him up quickly. He thumbed his phone to call Gideon.

"Hey, what's up?"

"Got a guy, a few inches shorter than you, in much better shape than you, black hair, clean cut, real professional looking, potentially headed your way."

"Got it. Tail him, but don't be too obvious. Lemme know if he heads to the infirmary. I've already got a deal going with the receptionist, so just let him do his thing."

"Hey," the charming professional greeted. "I was wondering if that young woman I dropped off earlier was all right?"

"Oh, of course," the receptionist said, trying to be casual. "Would you like to see her? She's just down there, in room 4."

"Thank you." The professional went down the corridor and found room 4. He saw Kiwi still passed out, with IV lines hooked up to her.

"Oi there, mate," a voice said from the back corner. "You wouldn't be Jason, would you?"

Jason snapped around to his back left to see Gideon, just as the door opened. Dax walked through, arms crossed. Philly Cheesesteak was right behind him. *"Hyehhhhhhhh!"* he hissed at Jason.

"Oh," Gideon said, standing up. "So you *are* Jason." He approached Jason, sizing him up. He was fit, but much shorter than Gideon, and Dax towered over both of them. "I take it you know who I am."

Jason knew he was trapped, and tried to calm his panic. He quivered his head, indicating he didn't know who Gideon was.

Gideon could tell it was the truth. He nodded. "Well, Jason, I appreciate your honesty, so let me be honest with you. Answer all of my questions as thoroughly as possible, and you'll be free to walk back to your ship and leave the station. We know where you're docked, so we know your ship. If you *don't* answer my questions, or if I'm not satisfied with your answers, my head of security, the gentleman standing right behind you, is gonna knock you out, throw you into a cart, roll you down to our own ship, and hang you up as his knew heavy bag, he's a bit of a boxer you see, and he's gonna practice his body shots on you until I *am* satisfied."

He gave Jason a second to absorb that before saying, "Now, was all of that clear? Do you have any questions before we get started?"

Jason's throat was paralyzed. He shook his head, indicating that he had no questions.

Back on the *Isle of Skye*, Kiwi couldn't eat fast enough. "Thanks for grilling up the steak, Dax," she said through a mouthful of ribeye and roasted corn. "God bless you East Texas hicks, this is fucking delicious."

"Slow down, Rosevine, or you're gonna get an upset stomach and puke it all up, and I'm *not* making you another one."

Kiwi rolled her eyes. "Yes, *dad*."

Gideon strolled into the mess hall to find the two of them: three of them when he noticed Philly Cheesesteak at Kiwi's feet, seemingly guarding her. "Oi, how the three of you doing? Glad I got you all together."

Kiwi kept her eyes on her plate while Gideon approached, still feeling shameful about what happened. "You're not gonna scold me in front of everyone, are you?"

"No, love," Gideon said, sitting down. "I think you understand now why I asked you to stay onboard."

Kiwi nodded sheepishly.

"And I think if I ask you to do something from now on, that you're gonna do it."

Kiwi nodded again. "I'm sorry, guys. Thanks for saving my ass."
Philly Cheesesteak head-butted her leg and purred.

"You should thank Philly Phil," Dax said. "He's the one who found you and sniffed out the guy that kidnapped you."

"Thank you, Philly Phil," she said, her tone of voice still down.

"Stop sulking," Gideon said. He thumbed his phone. "Take a look at your phone, just transferred your share of the Easter Egg heist."

Kiwi pulled out her phone and gawked. "What the fu…"

"See, both of you were making fun of me for running out to Uranus to steal a bunch of eggs, until you saw the payday."

"I mean, I was gonna make a Uranus joke, but…" Kiwi said.

"Well," Gideon said, thumbing his phone back up and sending Kiwi and Dax some info. "Queue up your best Mars jokes, because that's where we're headed next."

Dax and Kiwi both looked at their phones, but were confused. "If we're headed to Mars, why'd you send us a bunch of resumes?" Dax asked. "What's the job?"

"Oh god," Kiwi said. "We're not hiring someone else, are we?"

"*I*," Gideon emphasized, "am hiring someone else who has a skill set all of us lack and that we'll need. So to answer your question, Dax, the job is to go through these resumes and pick out your three favorites. Decide who you like by tonight, because we're doing interviews tomorrow."

"What are we looking for?" Dax asked.

"We need a sniper," Gideon said.

"What the fuck, we're not assassins, Gideon," Kiwi said.

"Well it's a good thing our next job doesn't involve killing anyone," he said. "Let's just say it involves Mars, rally car racing, legal and illegal gambling, and a sniper."

Dax's confused look suddenly turned to understanding. "Oh, we're going to Le Mons?"

Gideon nodded. "Decide tonight who you like. We interview them tomorrow." He left the mess.

Kiwi looked at Dax. "The fuck is Le Mons?"

"You know, named after Olympus Mons? Biggest mountain on Mars?"

Kiwi was still confused.

"It's a play on the classic *Le Mans* race they've held in France for hundreds of years?"

Kiwi's face was blank.

"Bunch of Mars colonists started their own race and called it 'Le Mons' and it's become the biggest rally car event in the solar system for the last 80 years, and it pisses off the *Le Mans* people because *Le Mans* isn't rally car racing?"

Kiwi shrugged.

Dax sighed. "Let's just look at these goddamn resumes."

8. Noora, Finnish Sniper

Kiwi hates women, and the team interviews a new crew member.

"No!" Kiwi insisted. "We are *not* hiring a fucking woman!"

"First of all, *I* am hiring whomever I goddamn want," Gideon said. "And second, we haven't even interviewed her yet."

"Yeah, what's wrong?" Dax asked. "You don't trust your own kind?"

"Dax, I hate working with women even more than you hate asking them out," Kiwi said. "They *don't* wanna work, they're always late, they're always gossiping behind your fucking back, and they have *no* spatial awareness at all."

Dax raised an eyebrow and looked back at his phone. "Takes one to know one."

"That's my point!" Kiwi said.

"Well look," Gideon said. "We agree we don't like anyone else we've talked to."

"That last guy was okay," Kiwi said.

"*That last guy* was a strung out ex-Space Forcer with PTSD who needs therapy more than we need him," Gideon said.

Kiwi shrugged. "I mean, he was cute, though."

Gideon stood up, looking at his phone. "All right, she's almost here. I'm gonna go meet her at the airlock, then I'll bring her back here to the mess, so stay put." He moved for the exit, just as Philly Cheesesteak came through an air vent. "Oh hey, little Cheesesteak. Go hang out with the gang, I'll be right back."

"Br-r-r-r-ryeah," Philly Cheesesteak acknowledged.

Gideon sat at 12-o'clock, Dax at 3-o'clock, and Kiwi at 9-o'clock. Philly Cheesesteak stood on the table next to Kiwi, trying to be polite to their guest with his eye contact.

At 6-o'clock sat their guest: all of 5-foot-4-inches, cropped blonde hair tucked neatly behind her ears, and subtle makeup that accented her cerulean eyes. She wore a leather jacket, a ringed choker, denim jeans, and long leather boots.

Behind her sat a mountain of her own luggage and gear.

"So, you and I have met," Gideon said to their guest before turning to his crewmen. "You two mind introducing yourselves?"

Dax did a quick wave of his hand. "Dax. Ship's engineer, head of security, head chef, and the muscle, depending on what the captain needs."

"Dax, a pleasure," the guest said. "French?" she asked.

Dax did a quick double-take. No one had ever identified the etymology of his name. "I, um, I mean French first name, Spanish family name. Last name's Rodriguez."

The guest nodded. "I *thought* I had you pegged as Mediterranean."

"Don't let that fool you. He's an East Texas hick, in case his accent didn't give it away," Kiwi said. She gave her best resting bitch face. "Speaking of, where's *your* accent from? I can't place it."

"Oh, I'm Fennesh," the guest said.

It took Kiwi a second to comprehend. "Oh, you're *Finnish*?" she asked.

"Yup, from Fenlend," the guest confirmed. "And I'm sorry, I'm Noora, by the way, forgive my manners."

"Kiwi," Kiwi said. "Ship's alcoholic."

"Kiwi," Noora said, delighted. "I love the name."

Kiwi relaxed some of the bitch from her face, and managed to be polite for a second. "Thanks."

Noora looked at Philly Cheesesteak. "And who're you?"

Philly adjusted his posture, blinked his eyes, and politely looked away, pleased at being noticed.

"This is Philly Cheesesteak," Kiwi said. "He's my best friend, and he secretly runs the ship."

"Oh my gahd," a charmed Noora said, leaning onto the table and offering her hand. "Phelly Cheesesteak, can I say hi?"

Philly Cheesesteak strutted up to Noora, tail raised high, and head-butted her hand, purring loudly.

Noora scratched his head a few times then patted his back. "Gedeon," she said. "You said *you* were the captain. You're not misleading me, are you? This lettle dude seems to be in charge."

Gideon couldn't help a smirk. He tried to get the conversation back on track. "So, says on your resume that you're a biathlete."

"Oh, yeah," Noora said while she finished petting Philly Cheesesteak. "I mean, I was into that as a ked and into my teens, but then I joined the Fennesh army at 18, went to sniper school because I had the, you know, sharpshooting background through the biathlon. I never saw combat, but I was first in my class at sniper school."

Kiwi raised an eyebrow. "What does *that* mean?" she asked. "*First in your class at sniper school?*"

Noora didn't miss a beat. "Oh yeah, it means that I'm hiding in camouflage on a hill, with a rifle, and a sniper instructor stands within one meter of me, and the other sniper instructors try to spot me, knowing that I'm within a meter of the guy, but they stell can't see me. I was the only one in my class that did that."

That got Gideon and Dax's attention.

Kiwi was skeptical. "Okay, so you can hide well, but can you *shoot* well?"

"Of course, I mean, not to brag, but I was relly good at biathlon. Your heart is *pounding* when you het the ground and start hetting your targets. I mean sniper school was easy after that, because you just set for hours, hedden away, heart nice and steady." She fanned herself. "I'm sorry," she said, removing her leather jacket. "Can I take this off, it's warm in here."

Dax and Gideon managed to hide their gawking.

Kiwi didn't. "Holy fucking shit," she said. "You're cut."

Noora wore a leopard-print tank top under her leather jacket, exposing her arms and shoulders. "Oh, thank you," she said. "Yeah, of course I was in shape when I did biathlon, but after I stopped, like, I needed some other form of exercise, and I pecked up weightlifting and I just got addicted to it. And, you know, being out in space for a long time, it's good to strength train all you can."

"Can you, like, flex?" Kiwi asked.

Noora smiled. "You want me to flex? Sure." She held up her arms and flexed. Her physique was carved from ivory.

"Guys," Kiwi said. "You can see her abs through her fucking tank top."

Philly Cheesesteak head-butted Noora's hand, demanding more pets. Noora cooed at him and obliged.

"So," Gideon said, trying to take control of the interview, "you're a good shot?"

"Yeah, I mean, I wasn't sure what you were looking for, so I brought all my gear weth me to give you a demonstration if you needed," Noora said, pointing a thumb at the mountain of luggage behind her.

"What do you have?" Dax asked, interested.

"Just long rifles and pestols," Noora said. "Like, I've got a classic Mosin-Nagant, and a—"

"Whoah," Dax interrupted. "You've got an original Mosin-Nagant?"

"Careful, Noora," Kiwi interrupted. "I think Dax likes you."

Noora found Kiwi's tease endearing. She smiled. "I also have a powered Henry lever-action in .45-70, it's basically a torpedo launcher, it's my favorite."

Gideon nodded, thinking of his lever-action katana.

"But," Noora continued, "my crown jewel is a Remy-Larsson Liminal."

Dax and Gideon both gawked openly this time.

"What's, I mean, what's 'liminal'?" Kiwi asked. "Is that Finnish for something?"

"No, I'm pretty sure that's English?" Noora said, suddenly skeptical of her second language skills. "But yeah, it's basically a ship cannon they converted into a rifle. It's got a convertible barrel for just about any round, but it can fire a .22-size slug at 5% the speed of light."

Kiwi rolled her eyes. "Wow," she mocked, still trying to antagonize Noora, and still failing. "A whole .22?"

"At 15,000 kilometers a second," Noora confirmed. "I mean, you basically need a separate power source to shoot the thing, and it's clunky, but holy shet, at that speed it goes *exactly* where you want."

Gideon's mind was made up, but he polled his two crewmen to let them at least think that he would weigh their opinions. "Any last questions for Noora before we have her give us a demonstration?"

"Oo, I have a question," Kiwi said. "Noora, in your opinion, why can't Dax get laid?"

Dax, arms crossed, rolled his eyes to the ceiling. Gideon face-palmed himself.

But Noora took the question in stride. She gave Dax a thorough look. "I mean, with arms like that, I'm surprised you're not fighting off every woman on the station, to be honest."

Kiwi's mouth dropped, and she pointed at Noora. "Yes!" she exclaimed. "Thank you! You see, Dax, you *can* get laid, and I'm not the only one who thinks so."

"How tall are you, by the way?" Noora asked Dax. "6-4?"

"6-2," Dax said.

"Dax, Jesus Christ," Kiwi said. "If a woman asks you if you're 6-4 you say 'yes'!"

"But I'm 6-2."

"Women don't understand the fucking difference!" Kiwi tried to explain. "From now on, you're 6-4!"

Gideon, face still in his palm, quietly asked, "How 'bout you, Dax? Any questions for Noora?"

"Yeah," Dax said, arms still crossed. "What do you know about rally car racing?"

Noora scoffed cutely. "Are you serious? I'm Fennesh. We love rally cars. I was actually hoping to make it to Mars for the Le Mons, since that's happening soon, but I go where the jobs are."

Dax gave Gideon a look that said 'hire her now,' before Gideon said. "All right. Let's head to the armory. Show us what you got."

"Rifles are too easy," Kiwi said. "Let's see what you can do with a pistol."

Dax and Gideon knew Kiwi had a point, but were getting annoyed with her attitude.

But Noora wasn't. "You know. You're absolutely right," she said, pulling out a small-caliber pistol.

"Oh wow," Kiwi mocked. "Another .22?"

Noora snapped in a magazine, aimed down the range, and unloaded the entire clip in about five seconds. She called the target back, showing a hollowed out bullseye.

"Yeah," Kiwi said, pretending to be unimpressed. "But can you handle something that kicks?"

"Hey," Noora said, flexing again. "Have you seen these guns? Because these guns can handle *any* gun."

Gideon pulled out his revolver and handed it to Noora. "See what you can do with that," he said.

"Oooo," Noora said, recognizing the make. "A fellow Remy-Larsson connoisseur." She checked the twin barrels, cocked it, and let loose all 12 rounds at another target.

"Fuck, Gideon," Dax said. "She's a better shot than you."

"This is so fucking cool," Noora said, admiring the revolver. She handed it back to Gideon and said, "Thank you for that."

"Thank *you*," Gideon said. "You're hired. When can you ship out?"

"Right now," Noora said. "I mean that pile of stuff is my gear *and* my luggage."

Kiwi casually strolled off, saying, "Whatever, Gideon. You wanna hire another woman, that's on you."

Again, Dax and Gideon rolled their eyes up to the ceiling.

"I'm sorry," Gideon said. "Kiwi's really great, but she can be a real, well, you know."

"Are you kidding?" Noora said, delighted. "She and I are gonna be besties."

9. A Finnish Sniper on The Isle of Skye

Gideon tells the crew their next job, Kiwi thinks the plan is stupid, Dax does some math, and Noora snipes something 1000 kilometers away.

"All right, kids," Gideon said in his Scottish cadence. "Let's go over the job."

Kiwi, Dax, Noora, and Philly Cheesesteak all sat at a table in the mess hall, waiting for details.

"We're obviously heading to Mars, in case you didn't know that already, and we're playing a key role in the upcoming Le Mons race."

"Holy shet!" Noora exclaimed in her Finnish accent. "We're not racing in Le Mons, are we? Oh my gahd, I've always wanted to go!"

"Calm down, sugar tits," Kiwi said with her Wisconsin passive-aggression. "We're not racers."

"You didn't even know what rally car racing was until 5-minutes ago," Dax pointed out in his East Texas drawl.

"Mr-r-r-reh," Philly Cheesesteak concurred.

"I said we're not racers, Dax, was I fucking wrong!" Kiwi countered.

"Jesus Christ," Gideon interjected. "Everyone calm down. You're right, Kiwi, and Noora I'm sorry to give you the bad news, but we're not racing. We're actually gonna sabotage it."

"I'm sorry," Noora said. "What?"

"What?" Dax said.

"Fucking what?" Kiwi said.

"Br-r-reh?" Philly Cheesesteak said.

"Noora," Gideon said. "You're the one that's gonna pull this off, but it's gonna take all of us."

"Holy shet," Noora said. "Did you hire me to, like, fucking snipe some drivers?"

"No," Gideon said. "Just a tire."

Noora frowned in confusion. So did Dax and Kiwi.

Gideon continued. "Big racing event, there's shitloads of legal and illegal gambling, and we're gonna get a piece of it. Or at least that's what our employer is telling me."

"Who's this *employer*?" Noora asked.

"It's a gentleman who finds jobs and contracts for mercenaries like us," Gideon said.

"And the job is to shoot out a fucking tire?" Noora asked.

"Yeah," Dax said. "Gideon, I'm just as lost as she is. What *exactly* is it we're supposed to do?"

"We just need to make sure a certain racer doesn't finish in the top three."

"Oh no," Noora said. "Not Edvard!"

Gideon nodded.

"Oh wait, Edvard Raikkonen?" Dax asked.

Gideon nodded again.

"Okay, now *I'm* lost," Kiwi said.

"He's, like, the best rally car driver alive," Dax said. "He's won Le Mons three times in a row and he's favored to win again."

"But he's Fennesh, just like me!" Noora said. "I can't shoot my own countryman, Gideon!"

"You're not shooting *him*," Gideon repeated. "You're shooting out his tire."

"It's the principle of it!" Noora exclaimed.

Kiwi was frowning. "I'm sorry, so we need to shoot out a tire at a race just so some Finnish asshole doesn't place?" she asked. "This sounds really fucking dumb, Gideon."

"Well guess what, Rosevine, it's what we're doing."

"I mean she's right, man," Dax said. "Why not just slap a small explosive to a tire and bust it when we want? Or why not sabotage a timing belt or the brake hydraulics?"

"Because," Gideon said. "Even if you could get to the car itself, which you can't because they're under lock-and-key and they don't let just anyone near them, they run sweeps on the vehicles because people try to sabotage races all the time."

Kiwi rolled her eyes. "But shooting out a tire? Come on. Why don't we, like, just slip something in Edvard What's-His-Name's drink the night before and give him explosive diarrhea for a day?"

"Won't do," Gideon said. "He needs to be in the race, not out of commission, so that all the betting swings in the right direction. Then a nicely timed blowout ruins a bunch of gamblers' lives and gets us a nice payday."

He put his phone down on the table so it could project a presentation against the wall.

"There are 12 legs to the race, and you rally fans know each leg lasts a day." He went to the next slide. "Our problem is this; we need it to look plausible. If it's obvious sabotage, all the gamblers out there raise hell with the bookies, and we don't get a penny. So, we need it to look natural."

"And shooting out a tire is natural?" Dax asked.

"Blowouts aren't uncommon," Gideon said. "These guys don't use solid rubber tires. They're pressurized, which makes them vulnerable in the thin Martian atmosphere. We need to blow out one of Edvard's tires at the right moment in the right leg. And Noora, you're gonna use your Remy-Larsson Liminal to do it."

Noora's jaw was on the floor. "Holy shet," she said.

Kiwi raised a hand.

"What is it, Rosevine?" Gideon asked.

"This is dumb, Gideon," she said. "I don't care how good a shot she is. No sniper is hitting a tire on a rally car going at 90-miles-an-hour."

"I mean it shouldn't be difficult," Noora said. "That rifle can fire a .22 at 5% the speed of light, so the bullet is there instantly, it's just you need a power source the size of a tank."

"And lucky enough," Gideon said, "we've got two engineers to help you figure that out."

"Well," Dax said, "more like one-and-a-half engineers."

"Is that a joke about my size?" Kiwi asked. "Or is it because I don't have a degree?"

"Both," Dax said.

"I know everything you do, jackass," Kiwi shot back.

"Get a degree first, and *then* you'll be an engineer," Dax said.

Kiwi just rolled her eyes.

Gideon continued to the next slide. "Noora, you'll need to be in a blind on Olympus Mons itself, but I trust you'll know how to set that up given your experience. It's big enough so you can find an unoccupied spot where no one will see you, but again, I don't wanna take any chances."

"I mean, that's all well and good, but the Liminal takes so much power," Noora said.

"That's why you're gonna work with Dax and Kiwi," Gideon said. "Figure out how much power you need, how big a power source it's gonna take, and what you can safely transport and hide."

"How much time we have?" Dax asked.

The race starts in two weeks, we'll be there in one," Gideon said. "So you got a week, because once we get there, we need to scout out a spot and get set up, and that'll take longer than we want."

"That's why you need to learn the math, Kiwi!" Dax shouted, his hands and arms covered in grease.

"Yell at the fucking computer, Dax!" Kiwi shouted back, her hands and arms also covered in grease.

Dax rubbed his forehead, not caring how much grime he was getting on his face. He calmed his voice down. "Did you run the differential equation yourself?"

"You see, you use these words like 'differential,' and 'equation,' and my alcoholic ass doesn't understand," Kiwi said. "I understand things like 'plugging it into the computer,' and 'letting it come up with the required amount of wire insulation.'"

"Look," Dax said, rummaging through the mess of wires on their makeshift power source. "You're great with technical shit, and you're a natural mechanic, and this is where you need the math. I can tell you right now there's not enough insulation on these wires."

Kiwi scoffed. "Like hell."

Dax glared at her. "How much does a .22 bullet weight?"

Kiwi shrugged. "Not a lot?"

"How many Newtons is it hitting with at 5% the speed of light?"

Kiwi shrugged again.

"And when you know that, you know how much power needs to run through these wires, and how much insulation you need," Dax pointed out.

Noora walked into engineering, carrying an oversized case. "Hey you two," she said, plopping the case down, and showing off her physique while doing it. "I figured you'd need the rifle, so here it is."

"Yes," Dax said. "Thank you."

"Anything I can do to help?" Noora asked.

"Yeah," Kiwi said. "You can get me a beer, and you can tell Dax to stop worrying so much."

Gideon chimed in on the comm. *"Oi, all of you, get up to the bridge now."*

The three of them looked at each awkwardly for a moment, then all left engineering and made their way to the bridge.

"It's about 1000 kilometers away, hiding in what they think is a sensor shadow," Gideon said. "They've been stealthy about it, but there they are, clear as day."

"Oh shit," Dax said, looking at the viewscreen. "That's Jason's ship."

"Exactly," Gideon said.

"I'm sorry," Noora said. "Who's Jason?"

Kiwi answered. "He's a guy I tried to pick up, but he drugged me, captured me, and I poisoned myself when he tried to interrogate me, and Gideon and Dax made him piss his pants."

"And looks like he's been following us since we left Titan," Gideon said.

"I don't like him following us," Dax said.

"Neither do I," Gideon said. "Any suggestions?"

"I mean," Noora chimed in. "I could take some pot-shots at him with the Liminal."

"He's a thousand klicks away, sweetie," Kiwi said.

"Yeah," Noora said. "My scope can see that far, he's on the same trajectory as us, and, I mean, I'll have to get outside the ship and set up properly, but it should be easy."

Gideon checked in with Dax. "Is that possible?"

"I mean, a thousand klicks away, and firing at 5% the speed of light," Dax said, doing some quick mental calculations. "From the time she pulls the trigger to the time it hits them will take 1/15 of a second."

"Will it actually cause any damage?" Gideon asked.

"Well," Dax said, doing some more mental math, "yeah it's just a .22, but at that speed it'll be hitting with the force of a car doing 75-miles-per-hour." He looked at Kiwi and said, "And *that's* why you need to know your math."

"I love it," Gideon said. "Kiwi, get suited up and go with Noora. You'll need to set up outside the ship on the hull."

"For Chrissake," Kiwi said. "It's after 1700 hours, and I haven't have my first beer yet, so—"

"So get yourself suited up and help her," Gideon repeated.

Kiwi rolled her eyes and made for the exit. "I'll meet you up in the cargo bay, sweet tits."

After Kiwi left, Noora sheepishly went up to Gideon and quietly said, "So, Gideon, I know you hired me to be a sniper, but I've never, you know, actually killed anyone."

Gideon couldn't help a smile. "Don't worry, I'm not asking you to. Just target their engines, maybe their communications, anything that looks unoccupied."

Noora nodded, then made her way to the cargo bay.

Gideon looked at Dax. "What you do think?"

"I think," Dax said, "we're about to see what our Finnish sniper is really made of."

Clad in a pressure suit, Noora lay prone against the outside of the *Isle of Skye,* her Remy-Larsson Liminal rifle in hand, surrounded by the vacuum of space.

Kiwi was next to her, also clad in a suit, fumbling with connecting the rifle to the *Isle's* power.

"Not to rush you," Noora said through the shortwave radio. *"Just wanted to ask how that connection's going."*

"Just, gimme a sec," Kiwi said. *"This suit's gloves, I may as well be wearing Dax's boxing mitts."*

"Take your time," Noora said. *"I got them in my sights and they're not going anywhere."*

Kiwi finally got the connection in place. *"There, give it a go."*
Noora checked the heads-up-display on the Liminal. Everything was clear. She tuned up the power up to 5% the speed of light.

"Hey you two," Gideon chimed in from the bridge. *"How's it looking?"*

"Got them in my sights," Noora confirmed. *"Permission to fire, Captain Gideon."*

"Fire at will."

Noora pulled the trigger. A small, violet light flashed silently from the muzzle, and 1/15th of a second later, the .22 caliber bullet slammed into Jason's ship with 34,000 Newtons of force, 1000 kilometers away.

"Holy fucking shit," Kiwi said, admiring the Finnish sniper's work.

Noora smiled. *"Gideon, Dax, can you confirm any damage to their ship?"* she asked.

"Yeah," Dax answered. *"You definitely hit the engine compartment. They're leaking plasma exhaust."*

"Feel free to hit them again," Gideon said.

Noora aimed down the sights and was about to pull the trigger, when she looked at Kiwi and said, *"Would you like to give it a shot?"*

"Holy shit, yes."

Noora, staying connected to the hull, moved aside, and let Kiwi take the rifle.

"All right," Noora said. *"You should see them just looking down the scope."*

"Yeah," Kiwi confirmed. *"Jesus, I can't believe you can see them at a thousand klicks."*

"And just focus in on where you want to hit, and pull the trigger."

Kiwi salivated a bit at what she was about to do. She pulled the trigger, and saw through the scope the damage she'd done.

"Nice," Gideon chimed in. *"Another hit to their engines."*

"Oh, that wasn't me—" Noora started to say, before Kiwi pulled the trigger another half-dozen times.

"Heh-heh-heh-heh-heh-heh," Kiwi giggled.

"Holy fuck," Noora said.

"Holy fuck," Gideon echoed. *"That's good, that's good. I want to cripple them, not rip them apart."*

Kiwi got up, her magnetic boots keeping her stuck to the hull. *"Thanks,"* she said to Noora.

Noora laughed. *"You're a natural. We should practice together in the armory. I'll bet you'd love my other rifles."*

"Yeah, that'd be cool."

They gathered up the equipment, making sure none of it floated away into space, and made their way back to the cargo bay.

"So, uh," Kiwi said awkwardly. *"You wanna, like, have a beer in the mess?"*

"I'd love to," Noora said.

10. A Finnish Sniper on Mars

Noora does Kiwi's makeup, Kiwi picks up the right guy for the wrong reason, Gideon sits in a hotel, and Dax is too distracted to notice a fried battery.

"Where's Kiwi and Noora?" Gideon asked.

"I don't know," Dax said, scruffing his long hair. "They're probably playing dress-up or something."

"Are you serious?" Gideon asked. "They're actually getting along?"

"Yeah," Dax said. "Where've you been? They've been hanging out ever since they shot up Jason's ship."

Gideon dialed up his phone. "Well wherever they are, they're getting their arses to the bridge right away."

"You know," Noora said in her Finnish accent, straddling Kiwi's lap and carefully applying eyeshadow, "I relly love how you do your eye-liner and mascara."

"Thank you," Kiwi said, holding still while Noora applied eyeshadow. "I know I've got this goth girl thing going, but it just works."

"No, you're right!" Noora insisted. "It totally does! I just, I relly think adding this bet of penk to your eyeshadow would look so cute." She kept applying the eyeshadow, and changed the subject. "Hey, can I ask, you and Dax always seem to fight."

"Oh yeah," Kiwi said. "That's nothing. He's like, I don't know, he's like a big brother. He means well, and he has my back. I just like giving him shit because I know how guys relate to each other."

"So you and Dax. aren't, like, a thing?" Noora asked.

Kiwi pulled her face back skeptically. "Do you *like* him?"

"I mean," Noora stalled, applying more eyeshadow. "He's handsome, don't you think?"

"Eewww!" Kiwi said. "No!"

"Come on," Noora said. "With arms like that…"

Kiwi scoffed. "Girl, if you want your legs up on his shoulders, go for it. Trust me, he needs to get laid."

Noora lifted a coy eyebrow. "Just didn't want to step on anyone's toes." She finished up her eyeshadow work. "There," she said. "Have a look."

Kiwi looked in the mirror. "Holy fuck," she said, admiring the black eyeliner with the pink eyeshadow. "That's hot."

"Right?" Noora said. "I told you, just a little bet of penk, and it's super cute!"

Both of their phones chimed.

"Oi, both of you," Gideon chimed in. *"Get to the bridge with me and Dax. We're almost in Mars orbit. Got some details to go over before we drop to the surface."*

"And you're sure you can transport the thing?" Gideon asked.

"Oh yeah," Dax said. "We don't need the Liminal to fire at its max output of 5% the speed of light. Besides, even after popping a tire, that'd leave a huge. obvious crater. Only expect we'll need half a percent, which cuts way down on how much power we need, meaning a much smaller battery."

Gideon looked at Noora. "And you're sure that's all you'll need."

Noora nodded. "Oh yeah. I mean, even at half a percent the speed of light, that's, what is that?" she asked, looking at Dax.

Dax ran the quick math in his head. "1,500 kilometers a second."

Gideon whistled, impressed. He looked back to Noora. "And you got everything you need for the blind?"

"Oh yeah," Noora said. "I mean, people set up camp all over Olympus Mons to watch this thing, but like you said, it's the size of Poland, so there also won't be anyone near us. We can set up easily, find cover, and make the shot."

"Good," Gideon said, stroking his black beard. "I'm thinking we take the dropship to West Olympus, then Dax and Noora you two take the dropship to Olympus Mons along the west side, with a plan to snipe Edvard's car aiming southwest of there. Unless, of course, you think you need Kiwi to join you."

"No," Kiwi stated. "That battery we made weighs as much as I do."

"Which isn't much," Dax interjected.

"Exactly!" Kiwi interjected back. "There's no way I'm hanging out on that cramped dropship. Besides, Dax is the real engineer, and I need to be in West Olympus, where there are bars and nightclubs, and who knows, maybe I'll even get into the Le Mons pre-party."

Gideon scoffed. "That's invite-only."

"Gideon," Kiwi said, " you don't get it. Guys have to actually *be* somebody to get into a party like that. Girls like me just have to have perky boobs and a bubble butt, and I don't know if you've noticed, but I've got both."

Noora laughed.

Dax tried not to laugh.

"Hey, if you can get in, be my guest," Gideon said before standing up. "Anyway, let's all grab what we need and meet at the dropship in an hour."

It was a short hop from the West Olympus settlement to their chosen spot on Olympus Mons. They had just dropped off Gideon and Kiwi, and Dax was his stoic self while piloting.

"Thanks for putting the battery together, and the backup," Noora said.

"Yeah, of course, it's what I do."

"It was just relly brilliant of you to tune it down to just half a percent," Noora said, trying not to fawn over him.

"I mean," Dax said, trying to sound nonchalant. "It made sense. Only way we could get a power source small enough to hook up to that thing. Besides, it freed up enough materials to make the backup battery, too." He pivoted the drop ship to get ready to land.

"Oh," Noora said, putting her suit helmet on. "We landing?"

"Yup," Dax said. "This spot good?"

"Yeah, this looks like where we talked about. Lemme get out the Liminal when we land, scope things out."

As the dropship landed, scattering a metric ton of red, iron-oxide, Martian dust, Noora said, "I stell can't believe you guys hired me to shoot out Edvard Raikkonen's fucking tires."

"Kiwi!" Kiwi shouted, martini glass in hand, writhing to the night club music in the light Martian gravity, clad in a dark grey, tight-fitting one-piece that showed off her figure.

"What?" the blonde-haired pretty boy shouted back.

"*Kiwi!*" she shouted again. "You know, like the fruit! Like the bird!"

"Oh, yeah, Kiwi! That's a relly cute name!" the guy shouted back.

Kiwi was already tipsy, but still had her flirting faculties about her. "You're so cute! Your accent! It reminds me of my friend! She's Finnish!"

"Oh relly?" the guy said back. "I'm Fennesh, too!"

"*Oh my god!*" Kiwi shouted back. "What a small world!"

"Well, I mean, it's Mars, so it is small," the guy said back, trying to impress her with a bad joke.

Kiwi laughed, feeling confident in her black eyeliner and pink eyeshadow that Noora had applied earlier. "So what's *your* name!"

"I'm Edvard!" the guy said. "Raikkonen! Edvard Raikkonen, I'm racing in Le Mons starting tomorrow!"

The name rang a bell with Kiwi, but she was too tipsy to remember, and too flirtatious to care. "I've, have I heard of you before? That sounds familiar!"

Edvard laughed, thinking Kiwi was just a victim of girlish innocence. "I mean, I've won the race a few times, and the race starts tomorrow, so, you know…"

"I'm so embarrassed, I like, don't even follow racing!" Kiwi said.

Edvard scoffed playfully. "Then what are you even doing here? This is the pre-race party! Invite only!"

"It was easy!" Kiwi said, closing the short distance between them, still doing her hypnotic dance. "The guy at the door took one look at me and was like, 'you're in'."

Edvard smiled. "Well I'm glad he let you in!"

"Me, too!" Kiwi put her arms up on his shoulders, martini still in hand, still swaying to the music, and still holding his gaze. After about ten seconds, Edvard was hypnotized.

"Where are you staying?" he asked.

Kiwi leaned into his ear and said, "Well, here's what I'm thinking, Sir Eddie. Why don't you and I get a bottle of whatever they call Champagne here on the Red Planet, and go back to wherever *you're* staying?"

The next morning, Gideon felt mildly guilty for sitting in the comfort of a hotel room while Dax and Noora had spent the night cramped in the dropship and dealing with the constant, irritating red dust of Mars. Even the best air filters and magnetic sweepers never got rid of it all.

He had the TV screen on and tuned into the start of the Le Mons race. He pulled out his phone to ring up Dax. "Hey," he greeted. "You guys all set out there?"

"Yeah," Dax answered. *"Noora's already hanging out in the blind. You should see it. I'm here in the dropship, I know where she is, and even I can't see her."*

"I had a good feeling about her," Gideon said. "The rifle hooked up? Everything else looking good?"

"Yeah," Dax confirmed. *"The Liminal is hooked up to the battery, everything tests out good, and she tells me she's got a clear view of where the cars are supposed to come around on this leg. She's only got about five-degrees of visibility, but from what she's telling me, that's all she needs. I'm gonna join her in the blind in a bit, do a test fire, make sure it's all working."*

"Wonderful," Gideon said. "Need me to call you when they make the approach, or are you guys good?"

"Nah, we're good. We're tuned into the airwaves, we can hear the announcers. Just keep an eye on your TV. You'll know it when you hear about the blowout."

"Well then, Godspeed to you two," Gideon said.

Noora was lying prone and motionless in the blind, aiming her Remy-Larsson Liminal down the southwest corner of Olympus Mons.

Dax was with her, double-checking the battery and backup he and Kiwi had fabricated. *"About how far to the rally lanes?"* he asked over shortwave. Even in the blind, they were still in the thin Martian atmosphere, and had to wear suits.

Noora checked the heads-up display on her scope. It was awkward given she was looking at it through her suit helmet, but she read it clearly. *"86.27 kilometers,"* she said.

"And you can see through all the dust?" Dax asked.

"Oh yeah," Noora said. *"This scope is great. It's able to map everything in 3D and filter out any dust particles. Can see the rally lanes clearly."*

"Well, in that case, wanna give it a test fire? Make sure it works?"

"Can the battery handle it?"

"Oh yeah," Dax said. *"You'll be able to get about half a dozen shots off before it needs recharging, and we got a fully charged backup as well."*

"Well, in that case," Noora said, aiming at a boulder several kilometers away from the rally lanes. *"Targeting a boulder at 91.598 kilometers away, and firing."*

She gently pulled the trigger, and 0.06 seconds later, 91.598 kilometers away, a small boulder quietly exploded in the thin Martian atmosphere.

"Holy fucking shet," Noora exclaimed. *"Goddamn, this rifle is so fucking cool."*

Dax finally smiled. *"Where you get that thing, anyway? It's not something your typical civilian can afford."*

"Yeah, no shet," Noora said. *"Won it in the Saturn sniper challenge a few months ago. Whoever pings the most amount of visible rocks out of Saturn's rings wins."*

"And you won."

Noora suppressed a smile, even though she knew Dax couldn't see her face. *"I won."*

But Dax could hear the masked pride in her voice. He smiled again, distracted from the few ribbons of smoke coming from the battery.

Not that he would have noticed them in the dark blind. Nor could he feel the heat the battery was putting out between the frozen Martian surface and his insulated suit.

"About how much longer," Noora asked, still scouting the rally lanes down her scope.

Dax tuned his helmet frequency to the Le Mons broadcast. *"Sounds like they're about to start. Figure 20 minutes until they come around the bend."*

Gideon, watching the start of the race from the comfort of his hotel room, heard the announcer's comments, and immediately suspected foul play on Kiwi's part.

"And Edvard Raikkonen, looking really under the weather this morning, having a slow start off the line. People are wondering if maybe he came down with a cold overnight…"

He pulled up his phone and called her.

"Mmmm, yeah?" a drowsy Kiwi answered.

Gideon thought carefully about how to address her. He still felt guilty about shouting at her after their Easter Egg heist.

"Hey, Rosevine," he said calmly. "Just wanted to check in on you. How do you like your room?"

"Don't know," she said. *"I'm in someone else's room."*

"Oh," Gideon said, trying to act surprised. "Whose room are you in?"

"Oh man, it's this guy I met last night at that pre-Le Mons party, or whatever."

"So you did actually make it into the party?"

"Oh hell yeah. Anyway, he had to head off to the race, but he told me I could stay in his suite if I wanted to, and holy hell do I want to. This place is fucking huge, Gideon. And I get all the room service I want. I felt bad for the guy, though, I think he's more hungover than I am."

"No kidding," Gideon said, trying to sound casual. "Who is this guy, by the way?"

"Oh yeah, he's, um, Edvard-something-or-other? He's got Noora's accent. Edvard Riker-something? I don't know. Great guy."

Gideon's stomach dropped, but he kept his cool. "It wasn't, maybe, Edvard Raikkonen, was it?"

"Oh yeah!" Kiwi said. *"How did you know?"*

Gideon centered himself, trying to keep calm. "Kiwi, he's the guy whose tires we've been hired to shoot out."

There was a long pause on Kiwi's end. *"Oh,"* she finally said. *"Oh* that's *why I'd thought I'd heard his name before."*

"Kiwi," Gideon said calmly, politely, diplomatically. "Please tell me you didn't slip anything into his drinks last night?"

"You kidding?" Kiwi said. *"I didn't have to spike him with anything. He kept doing shots of red ale off my boobs, and by the way, I told him we should get some Champagne, but apparently they only have red ale on this fucking Red Planet. So anyway—"*

"Rosevine, Rosevine," Gideon interrupted. "It's fine, just wanted to check in on you."

"Oh," Kiwi said, pleasantly surprised. *"Okay, Gideon, well, I'mma enjoy this room service, so catch up with you later."*

"Of course, love," Gideon said. He hung up, then watched the race, hoping Dax and Noora could follow through, while feeling his blood pressure rise.

"So they're about to come around?" Noora asked.

"Yeah, but," Dax said, confused. *"Sounds like Raikkonen isn't in the lead? Sounds like he's behind everyone else."*

Noora, staring down her scope towards the rally lanes 86-kilometers away, frowned. *"Are you sure?"*

"Yeah, no, the announcers can't stop talking about it. Raikkonen's dead last," Dax said.

Noora raised her eyebrows, then focused down the scope. *"Well, at least I know who to aim at."*

A flurry of cars came around the rally lanes, directly down Noora's sights. She zoomed in on the last car.

"Yup," she confirmed. *"That's Raikkonen's car."* She curved her finger around the trigger.

"Whenever you're ready," Dax said.

Noora exhaled in her helmet, centering herself. She aimed slightly ahead of Edvard Raikkonen's left front tire, and squeezed the trigger.

But the Liminal didn't fire.

11. Three Black Eyes

Noora pulls a trigger, Dax gets two black eyes, Gideon gets one black eye, and Kiwi bares her fangs.

A flurry of cars came around the rally lanes, directly down Noora's sights. She zoomed in on the last one.

"Yup," she confirmed over shortwave. *"That's Raikkonen's car."* She curved her finger around the trigger.

"Whenever you're ready," Dax said.

Noora exhaled in her helmet, centering herself. She aimed slightly ahead of Edvard Raikkonen's left front tire, and squeezed the trigger.

But the Liminal didn't fire.

"Ummmm, Dax? It's not firing and I have no power."

Dax shined a light on the battery, finally seeing the ribbons of smoke coming out of it. *"Ah, shit shit shit shit shit,"* he said, scrambling to reconnect the rifle to the backup.

"What's wrong," Noora asked, still lying prone, aiming down the scope, and unable to see what Dax was doing.

"Battery's fried. It's fine, just hooking it up to the backup." He secured the rifle cable to the backup battery and switched it on. It immediately overheated, flashed

some smoke of its own, and died. *"No, no, no, what the fuck!"*

"Dax, what's wrong?" Noora repeated.

Dax's angry sigh was audible over the shortwave. "Both the main and the backup are fried. Whatever's wrong with them, I can't fix them out here."

"And he's gonna be outta my view in about 10 seconds," Noora said, looking down the rifle. *"So what do we do?"*

Dax exhaled. *"We head back to the dropship and tell Gideon we failed."*

Gideon, watching the race from the comfort of his West Olympus hotel room, saw that Dax was calling him, picked up his phone and said, "So, not to be a snarky arsehole, but you wanna tell me why Raikkonen didn't have a tire blowout just now?"

"Both the main and backup batteries are fried," Dax said. From the quality of the audio, Gideon could tell Dax was in his pressure suit. *"Test fire went fine, but the main fried after that. Fired up the backup, but that died as soon as I turned it on. No idea what the fuck's wrong with them. Hauling them back to the dropship now, don't know if I can fix them out here."*

"Damn," Gideon said, keeping one eye on the race. "I mean, look, Raikkonen's dead last. We might not even need to shoot a tire out."

"Yeah, but there are still plenty of legs left. He can come back and at least place, and that's what we're trying to prevent."

Gideon thought for a second, and had an idea. "Do what you can with the batteries. Keep me posted. Lemme see what I can do on my end."

"The hell you gonna do on your end?" Dax asked with a friendly jab. *"You're sitting in a hotel in West Olympus, for Chrissake."*

Gideon laughed, hearing Dax's frustrated humor. "Don't worry about it, mate. Lemme know about the batteries, and work with Noora on setting up another sniper spot."

"Aye aye, Captain."

They hung up, and Gideon quickly dialed up Kiwi's number.

"Holy shit," she answered. *"Twice in one morning, what can I do ye for, Sir Gideon?"*

"Hey, Rosevine, sorry to bug ya again," Gideon said. "You still in Raikkonen's hotel suite?"

"You're goddamn right I am," she said. *"Called room service, and I'm chowing down on the greasiest hangover breakfast right now. Thinking of turning in my notice to you and just becoming Raikkonen's sex slave."*

Gideon suppressed a laugh. "Yeah, and that's actually what I wanna talk to you about."

"God fucking dammet, Kiwi, you fucking fuck!" Dax shouted, rooting through the guts of the batteries back on the dropship.

"Jesus Christ, Dax, don't have an aneurysm," Noora said, trying to crack a joke. She tried in vain to brush some of the red Martian dust off her suit.

Dax took a breath, then sneezed from all the iron-oxide dust. "Sorry," he said. "It's just, I told her, I *told* her to check the insulation on the wires. Both batteries are all melted and fused up. There's no fixing them."

Noora took a breath herself. "So, what do you think we can do?"

Dax brushed his long hair back, feeling the grit of the Martian sand in it. "I mean, practically? Nothing," he said. "Sorry, I'm just irritated, tired, sick of being on this cramped dropship, and sick of this goddamn red sand."

"Well at least you're not sick of me," Noora said.

Dax's stoicism broke, and he managed a laugh. "No, no, you're awesome," he said. "I'm sorry, there's nothing I can do for the Liminal. You have any ideas?"

"Well," Noora said, going to her locker and pulling out a long item wrapped in burlap. "I brought my own backup, you know, just in case." She unrolled the burlap, showing its contents.

Dax's jaw dropped. "Holy shit. Is that your Mosin-Nagant?"

"That it is," Noora said, picking it up and racking the bolt.

"How the hell do you even have one?" Dax asked. "That's hundreds of years old."

"When this is done, we'll have a drink and I'll tell you about it," Noora said. "Right now, this is all we have if we want to blow out Raikkonen's tire."

Dax refocused, thinking about the ballistics of Noora's 19th-to-early-20th century rifle. "You got the original 7.62 ammo?" he asked.

"Of course," Noora said.

"What kind of range you think you can get on that thing?"

"Well," Noora stalled, not knowing how to answer the question. "I mean, a lot farther than on Earth. And almost no wind resistance."

Dax stood up. "Okay," he said. "I got an idea."

"Heyyy," Kiwi said, naked and slinking over a pillow, her rose vine tattoo on full display.

"Hey," Edvard Raikkonen said with a smile, walking into the hotel suite, suddenly forgetting his woes of the day at the sight of her. "I can't believe you're still here."

"Well, I mean," Kiwi said, rolling with the pillow, showing off her curves. "You *did* say I could hang out as long as I wanted, and I thought, you know, I could hang out until you got back."

"Well," Edvard said. "Now that I'm back, I hope that doesn't mean you're gonna leave."

Kiwi snuggled into the pillow while keeping his eye contact. "Does it look like I'm going anywhere?"

"Gideon, he's actually really cool," Kiwi said over the phone. *"I mean, he's a little awkward at times, but he's confident and holy shit does he have stamina."*

"How was he this morning?" Gideon asked.

"Oh god, this morning he was all like, 'Look, I don't care if I win or not, I just really feel connected with you, and you're so awesome,' and then he's asking if I'll fly back to Earth with him, and shit…"

"Okay," Gideon said. "This is good. How was he overall this morning?"

"Honestly, he's worse this morning than yesterday. Last night we kept talking, and drinking, and fucking—"

"That's more than I wanted to hear, love," Gideon interjected.

"Well don't ask for the details, then," Kiwi said back. *"Anyway, yeah, he was way groggier this morning than yesterday."*

"That's all I needed to know," Gideon said. "You still hanging out in his suite?"

"You kidding? This morning he told me not to leave. I mean I might actually hit the gym today, but I'm coming straight back here."

"Keep at it, love," Gideon said, before hanging up.

He rang up Dax and Noora.

"Sup captain?" Dax answered.

"Hey, Gideon," Noora said.

The background noise sounded like they were flying the dropship. "Hey you two. How are things?"

"We're headed to the southeastern part of Olympus Mons," Dax answered. *"Gonna try and get Raikkonen's car around that leg."*

Gideon scowled. "If the Liminal isn't working, what are you gonna get it with?"

"Some early 20th-century Russian bolt-action," Noora said.

Before Gideon could ask a follow up question, Dax said, *"So, Gideon, as badly as we're failing out here, you sound awfully relaxed. How come it sounds like you know why Raikkonen's in last place?"*

Gideon laughed, stroking his beard, thinking of how to phrase this. "Let's just say that not only did Kiwi get into the invite-only party, but she unwittingly seduced the right guy."

"Wait, oh my gahd!" Noora exclaimed. *"Is she hooking up with Raikkonen?!"*

"Yes," Gideon said. "She didn't even know it was him. She's been in his hotel suite for two nights now. And from the sound of things, she's ruining him properly. You two might not even need to make a shot."

"Well, we're heading down there anyway," Dax said. *"Let you know when we're set up."*

"That was really sweet of you," Noora said after they cut the call with Gideon.

Dax was confused. "What do you mean?" he asked, piloting the drop-ship.

"I mean, you know, it was Kiwi's fault the batteries failed, but you didn't mention that to Gideon."

Noora's comment made Dax pensive. He hadn't consciously thought about it, then found himself verbalizing why. "As much as it might seem like she and I don't get along, she's a good kid, and I'll never throw her under the bus. And as brazen as she is, she feels really guilty when she fucks up. When we're back on the *Isle*, I'll quietly remind her that this is why she needs to know her differential equations."

Noora smiled, letting out a brief, audible laugh.

Her smile infected Dax. "What's so funny?" he asked.

"Nothing," Noora said. "It's just, Kiwi said something similarly affectionate about you. You two are like siblings that pretend to hate each other."

Dax scoffed a quick laugh, seeing Noora's logic.

"Anyway," Noora said. "Tell me about this plan you have."

"Easy," Dax said. "Set up a new blind where you're facing the inside lanes, when Raikkonen comes around, you blast his tire."

"We're gonna have to be a lot closer," Noora pointed out.

"Well, it's a good thing you know how to hide."

Edvard Raikkonen entered his hotel suite, both dejected from the day's events, and elated at seeing his little Kiwi.

"Hey!" Kiwi greeted, running up to him, clad in a sports bra and matching underwear, knowing it had the same effect as the slinkiest lingerie.

"Hey you," Raikkonen smiled. Kiwi reached for him, and he said, "Whoah, I still have my suit on, and I'm covered in Martian dust.

Kiwi laid her arms on his shoulders and linked her fingers on the back of his neck. "Well, I'll tell you what," she said. "Why don't you get out of that suit, and then meet me in the shower?"

Raikkonen smiled again. Kiwi let go of him and swayed her hips towards the shower, slipping her bra and underwear off along the way, knowing full well Raikkonen was watching her the whole time.

"Ah, shit," Dax said over the shortwave. He was a couple hundred meters west of Noora's new blind, watching the rally cars approach the bend where Noora was set to take the shot.

"That doesn't sound good, Dax. What is it?" Noora's voice chimed over the shortwave.

Dax tuned his binoculars into the last two cars of the pack. Raikkonen was one of them, but he was being crowded into an outside lane. *"Raikkonen's in an outside lane, looks like he's fighting another car for inside position, but I don't think he's gonna get it."*

"Fucking Raikkonen!" Noora exclaimed. *"He's better than that!"*

"Not today he isn't," Dax said. The cars came into the bend and started their lazy drift into Noora's view. With Raikkonen in an outside lane, and masked by another car, Noora wouldn't get a clear shot.

"Yeah, fuck," she said. *"I can't hit him, Dax. That other car's in the way."*

"Goddamn fucking Kiwi," Dax swore to himself, though it was still audible to Noora. *"She fries the batteries, and now she's fried Raikkonen so much we can't get a shot."*

Noora snorted a giggle.

Dax heard it and smiled. *"What's so funny?"*

"Well, I mean, it's funny, don't you think? She shorts out the batteries by accident, and then by accident seduces Raikkonen and puts him out of commission."

Dax smiled again, appreciating the irony.

"Yeah, they're almost outta my sight, Dax. I can't get anything."

"Okay, go ahead and pack up. I'm gonna call Gideon and let him know." He went through the selections in his heads-up-display, summoning Gideon's number.

"Hey you two," Gideon answered from his hotel room. *"I see Raikkonen's still racing, so I take it you couldn't get a shot?"*

"I'm so sorry, Gideon," Noora said, racked with guilt. *"I know you hired me for this, and I couldn't get a shot."*

"It's actually all right," Gideon said. *"Announcers have been saying even if Raikkonen wins every other leg of this race, there's no way he's placing in the top three."*

Dax scoffed. *"So, we're good?"*

"Yeah, mate, we're good. Get your arses back to West Olympus."

Dax scoffed again as they hung up. *"Goddamn. Just like that."*

Dax had taken several showers and groomed himself thoroughly, but still felt like the Martian dust was all over him. He scratched his thin beard and raised his glass of bourbon. "To failure," he said.

Gideon raised his glass of scotch. "Hey, it wasn't you that failed, but why not, to failure."

They downed their glasses.

"By the way," Gideon said. "You figure out why both batteries failed?"

Dax nodded, taking a few seconds to think about how to respond. "Yeah. We honestly didn't test them enough. You gotta test these things to failure, and we didn't do that. Not to blame you, but we didn't really have enough time. Test fire went fine, but then everything after that failed."

Gideon brushed it off. "That's fine, mate," he said, motioning to the bartender for another round.

The bartender came up and poured another bourbon and scotch.

"So," Dax said. "Did we actually get a payout?"

"I mean, didn't exactly go as planned, but the end result was all the same, so yeah. We have Kiwi to thank for that."

"Hilarious," Dax said ironically, downing his bourbon. "So, what you say we get outta here?"

"We've barely had a few drinks," Gideon said, downing his scotch.

"Yeah, but this bar is loud, and I wanna get outta here," Dax said, feeling his introversion creep up on him.

"No problem, mate," Gideon said. He settled up their tab, and the two of them made their way out of the West Olympus bar. They didn't notice the figures following them. "Where's Kiwi and Noora, by the way?"

"I don't know," Dax said, strolling down the shipping lanes by all the airlocks, on their way back to the hotel. "Probably gossiping up back in their hotel room, or something."

They came up to a shipping lane by an airlock, when three figures stood out in front of them.

"The fuck you sweet pies want?" Dax asked, his tipsiness getting the better of him.

"Oh it's easy, my friends," a familiar voice said behind them. Gideon and Dax turned around to see an equally familiar face, backed by two more figures. "We want you to come with us. Quietly. Calmly. Coolly."

Dax pointed a finger at the man, then looked at Gideon and said, "The fuck is *he* doing here?"

"You're Jason, right?" Gideon asked. "We shot up your ship. What *are* you doing here?"

"So it *was* you," Jason said.

"Hey Jason, I gotta question," Dax said, having sized up the situation they were in, and being loaded up on enough booze to not care. "Which one of your boyfriends do you want me to fuck up the least?"

Dax, tied to a chair, both eyes black and mostly shut, spat a clot of blood on the floor.

Gideon, with only one black eye, looked over to his crewmate. "Hey," he said to his captors. "That's not fair. How come he's got two black eyes and I've only got one?"

The svelte Jason leaned in and said, "Because *he* gave us a lot more trouble than you."

"Hey," Dax said through his daze. "How is that one guy's liver? Jesus, he dropped when I popped him there."

"He's recovering," Jason said.

"And how's that fat fuck's jaw?" Dax asked.

"Broken."

Dax let loose a drunk, bloody giggle.

"Look," Jason said, trying to take control of the conversation. "Just so you two know what you're into, we're gonna extract everything we can from you, because you owe us some fucking answers about that Easter Egg heist of yours, and then we're gonna contact that little Kiwi of yours and get her to pay a ransom for you."

Dax started giggling harder. He looked towards Gideon, who also started giggling.

"You," Gideon said through his laughter. "You wanna tell him?"

"No, captain," Dax said. "Please. The honor is yours."

Jason was confused. "The fuck are you talking about?"

"I, uh, I don't think you know who you're dealing with," Gideon said, still laughing. "That *little Kiwi* is gonna come at you harder than you understand."

"He's right," Dax said in his East Texas cadence. "She needs about half an hour of sleep and a bottle of whiskey to fuck you over harder than you thought possible."

Jason scoffed, even though he saw the confidence in both of them. "Well," he said. "Let's call her and find out."

"I can't believe you slept with Raikkonen!" Noora exclaimed. "I mean, like, I shouldn't ask, but like, how *was* he?"

"Oh my god, he was great!" Kiwi said, taking a pull from her bottle of Twin Diesel bourbon. "I mean, he had this awkwardness about him, but I couldn't tell if that was, like, him being Finnish and me being Wisconsin, or what, but he was so sweet!"

"My gahd, you're so fucking cute. I just, I'm just, like, wow!"

"Speaking of," Kiwi said. "Soooo, how was all your time alone with Dax?"

Noora blushed and got shy. "I mean, we were out on the dropship the whole time, and I felt so shy, like, I hope he doesn't think I was trying to flirt with him…"

"Girl, trust me, he doesn't understand how girls flirt. Did he smile at all?"

"Oh yeah, quite a bit."

"Yeah," Kiwi confirmed. "He never smiles. He fucking likes you."

"Oh my gahd, do you, like, do you really think so?"

"I, just, trust me," Kiwi said, as her phone rang. It was Gideon's number. "Hey, cap'n. Sup?"

"This is not your captain speaking," a familiar voice said.

"What?" Kiwi said.

"Lemme tell what's up, cupcake," the voice said. *"We've got your two buddies here with us, and they're about to tell us everything we want to know, and if you want them back, you're gonna do exactly what I say."*

Kiwi bared her fangs. "I fucking know your voice. Did you steal my guys from me, you fucking fuck?!"

"Let's just say that—"

"Hey! Fuckhead!" Kiwi screamed. "*No* one steals my guys from me! You have any idea what's about to happen to you?!"

"You won't find your guys with that attitu—"

"You think I'm coming for my guys?! I'm coming for *you*! And I've got *alcohol* on my side, bitch! Alcohol is the most destructive force in the *fucking* universe! And it's my *fucking* ally! So I'm coming for you, fuckhead! I *know* who you are, and you have *no* idea what I'm about to *fucking* do to you!"

Kiwi hung up.

Noora stared, jaw agape.

Kiwi caught her breath, and said, "Sorry. So, uh, a situation has come up, and we need to save Gideon and Dax."

"Uhm," Noora said, awkwardly. "Okay?"

12. Half an Hour of Sleep and a Bottle of Whiskey

Kiwi uses the f-word 15 times, Noora finally gets to use her rifle, Dax can't see, Gideon gets his phone back, and no one knows what the word "Liminal" means.

"Hey! Fuckhead!" Kiwi screamed. "*No* one steals my guys from me! You have *any* idea what's about to happen to you?!"

"You won't get your guys back with that attitu—"

"You think I'm coming for my guys?! I'm coming for *you*! And I've got *alcohol* on my side, bitch! Alcohol is the most destructive force in the *fucking* universe! And it's my *fucking* ally! So I'm coming for you, you *fuck*! I *know* who you are, and you have *no* idea what I'm about to *fucking* do to you!"

Kiwi hung up.

Noora stared, jaw agape.

Kiwi caught her breath, and said, "Sorry. So, uh, a situation has come up, and we need to save Gideon and Dax."

"Uhm," Noora said, awkwardly. "Okay?"

Kiwi realized this required some backstory for the relatively new Noora. "Remember that ship we shot up with your Liminal?"

"Yeah, of course."

"Well, that's the guy that kidnapped me and tried to drug me, well actually I drugged myself and screwed up his plans, but we made him piss his pants and then sent him on his way. Anyway, he's got Gideon and Dax, and we're gonna save them."

"Okay," Noora said, still stunned by the situation. "So, what are we gonna do?"

Kiwi took the cap off her bottle of Twin Diesel bourbon and threw it on the floor, taking a hard pull. She ripped the bottle away from her mouth and exhaled sharply. "I don't know. Gimme, like, gimme like half an hour and come get me," she said, heading for one of the hotel room beds.

His mouth was bloody, both of his eyes were black and swollen shut, and Dax couldn't stop laughing. Gideon was giggling, too.

"What's so funny?" Jason asked, putting his phone away.

"You think we couldn't hear her screaming at you?" Dax asked. "You're fucked, my friend."

"Maybe not as fucked as you two are," Jason said, procuring a jet injector.

Gideon only had one black eye, so could see what was in Jason's hand. "Lemme guess," he said. "You're gonna inject us with something that'll make us tell you the truth."

The clean-cut Jason gave Gideon a stern look. "Exactly."

Gideon looked at Dax. "Oi, Dax. Remind me, how much did we drink at that bar?"

"I don't remember," Dax said, picking up on Gideon's tone. "I lost count after five."

A large figure behind Jason came up to him and said in his ear, "You know what happened last time. You can't inject them. Let them sober up overnight, make sure they're hydrated, and then you can inject them."

Gideon couldn't hear what was said, but knew it was in his favor. "Yeah," he said. "Listen to what your girlfriend said there, Jason."

Jason licked his lips, then bit them in frustration. "Fine," he told his henchman. "Leave them here, we'll interrogate them in the morning."

"Hey, um, Kiwi?" Noora said, gently shaking her crewmate.

Kiwi, mouth wide open and drool coming out, unconsciously smacked her lips.

Noora tried again. "Hey, Kiwi."

Kiwi snapped awake, taking a few seconds to orient herself. "Oh, hey, yeah," she said, drowsy.

"Hey, I'm sorry," Noora said. "It's been half an hour."

Kiwi squinted her eyes at Noora. "I'm sorry. I didn't mean to fall asleep."

"No, it's all right, it's just, I mean, so what do you think we should do?"

Kiwi took a huge breath, let it go, then grabbed her bottle of Twin Diesel, and took a pull. She ripped the bottle away and exhaled hard. Noora could smell the bourbon on her breath.

"Here's what we do," Kiwi said decisively. "We check out right now, grab the dropship, and get our cute little asses back to the *Isle of Skye*."

"Um, okay?" Noora said, feeling like the plan was incomplete. "And what do we do after that?"

"Don't worry," Kiwi said, standing up. "I'll figure that out later."

"All right!" Kiwi shouted through the dropship turbulence as they ascended through the thin Martian atmosphere. "Here's what we do! We double check on Philly Cheesesteak, and then we go to fucking bed!"

"Um, okay?" Noora shouted back, not sure what the plan was, or if there even was one. She could barely hear Kiwi through the turbulence, so dropped the subject.

As the dropship cleared the atmosphere and things became smooth, Kiwi asked, "Hey, you packed your Liminal rifle, right?"

"Oh yeah," Noora said. "We got it."

"Do you mind if I take a look at it later? After I've slept for a bit?"

"No, yeah, of course," Noora said.

The dropship came in to a lazy dock with the *Isle of Skye.*

Philly Cheesesteak recognized the sound through the bulkheads, and made sure to greet his crewmates at the airlock.

"Hey, Philly Phil!" Kiwi squealed.

"Br-r-r-reh!" Philly Cheesesteak grunted.

"Well it's nice to see you, too, asshole," Kiwi said, scratching his head. "The hell's your problem? I told you we'd be away for a few days."

"Meh," Philly Cheesesteak conceded.

"Hey Philly-boo," Noora greeted. Philly Cheesesteak came up to her affectionately, tail raised high, purring loudly. Noora scratched his head.

"Hey, um, is this the Liminal?" Kiwi asked, eyeing one of Noora's long, oversized bags.

"Oh, yup, that's the one."

"Cool if I take it?"

"Of course!"

"Thanks," Kiwi said. "I'm just gonna drop it in the armory for now, then I'm gonna get some sleep." She grabbed the bag and headed off to the armory, noticing that Philly Cheesesteak's eyes were happily closed, enjoying all the scratches Noora was giving him. "Fine," she said. "Go sleep with your aunt Noora."

Noora could hear the joke, and smiled at Kiwi.

Kiwi smiled back.

"Hey," Dax said, spitting out the iron and copper taste in his mouth. "That alcohol bit sounds important."

"Yeah," Gideon said, trying to move the stiffness out of his neck. "I'll bet it's the same shit they tried to inject Kiwi, but she was too drunk and it overloaded her. The more booze in our system, the better."

"How much longer you reckon we got until they can inject us with their truth serum?"

Gideon shrugged as best he could given his binds. "Who knows. Better question is how long's it gonna take Kiwi to do something, and what's she gonna do?"

"Don't worry," Dax said. "You heard her. You know her. She'll destroy whatever she has to to get to us."

"She better not destroy the *Isle*," Gideon said.

"Jesus Christ, don't jinx it," Dax said.

Kiwi, tinkering away in the armory, writhed to her industrial rock, screaming to the lyrics the whole time.

"Welllll, I gotta little problem in the Martian sticks!
cuz I got some freedom fighters all on my six!
but then I turnaround and pick off those lunatics!
with my boosted auto-rifle, cuz I'm a fuckin bitch!"

Noora wandered into the armory, drawn to it from the blasting music, still drowsy from having just woken up. "Hey, um, Kiwi!"

"So it's too fucking bad you got up in my face!
and now I've blasted your ass all into outer space!

"Hey, Kiwi!" Noora shouted again.

"All powdered to dust, that's right, leavin no trace!
Cuz I'm a motherfuckin bitch and I'm a motherfuckin ace!"

"Kiwi!" Noora shouted.

Kiwi finally looked up, lifting up her welding helmet, showing her face stained with black grease. "Oh hey!" she said, turning the music down.

"Kiwi, what the fuck have you done!"

"I mean, um, you know, it's uh, what?"

"My fucking rifle!" Noora shouted again. "You've completely stripped it down! How did you even do that?"

"Oh, it's easy, I just kind of, you know, took it apart."

"You can't take it apart on your own!" Noora said. "You have to have it serviced by Remy-Larsson directly!"

Kiwi shrugged her shoulders.

"I just," Noora stammered. "I mean can you even get it back together again?" she asked, looking at all the parts of her Liminal rifle strewn over the armory.

"Oh, dude, of course I can!" Kiwi said. "Look, get this, I've figured out how to turn this thing into a full automatic."

Noora's jaw dropped. "No! You can't! You can only fire, like, six shots per minute, or else the barrel warps, and everything overheats!"

"Well, *yeah,* but that's, like, out-of-the-box," Kiwi said.

"What do you mean, 'out-of-the-box'?" Noora asked.

Kiwi scowled. "What do you mean 'what do you mean out-of-the-box'? All guns come out-of-the-box, and then you modify them however the hell you want."

"Well how the hell are you modifying this!" Noora exclaimed.

Kiwi took off her welding helmet, and also took a breath. "Okay, so, basically, I'm piecing it back together with a liquid-cooling system that uses coolant directly from our engines, and if we tune it down to about 2% the speed of light, we can spit out all the .22s we want at full auto. Granted we'd have to divert most of our engine power to it, but it can work."

Noora's jaw was still on the floor. "And how is that supposed to help us?"

"Yeah, okay, so, your scope," Kiwi said, looking around the armory for the scope. "*There* it is. So your scope, right? Remember when we shot up Jason's ship?"

"Yeah?"

"Well, your scope keeps a log of everything you've aimed at. And I got the logs from Jason's ship. I got the make, model, and registry number, fucking everything. It's named the *Sentinel*. Unoriginal, if you ask me."

Noora shook her head. "And?"

"And," Kiwi said. "I know where they're parked in Martian orbit, and maybe we just kind of get close enough and threaten them with a good time."

Noora was still baffled, but could hear Kiwi's conviction. "Okay, I mean, is there anything I can do?"

"Actually, yes!" Kiwi shot away from her work bench, came up to Noora, and pointed to a corner of the armory. "You see that? Have you ever worked an ammo-printer before?"

"Um, no?"

"Oh, it's easy!" Kiwi said, shuffling Noora over to the ammo-printer. "Here are the primers, here's the bullet-grain selector, and here's the casing selector. Just punch them in, and let it fly. And print out all you can, because we'll need a lot of it. You run out of materials, just yell at me."

"Umm, okay?"

"Don't worry, girl, you got this," Kiwi said, slapping Noora's butt, turning up the industrial rock and heading back to her work station. "Hey, what does 'Liminal' mean, anyway?" she shouted back at Noora.

Noora shrugged her shoulders. "No idea. I speak three languages, I don't have time to know what 'Liminal' means."

"Goddammet," Dax said, eyes still swollen shut, mouth still full of copper and iron. "I'm thirsty."

"Yeah, that's good," Gideon said, squirming in his binds. "Me, too."

"Why's that good?"

"Because the more dehydrated we are, the worse that drug will work," Gideon said. "It's like what they tried to do to Kiwi, only she was too drunk and dehydrated, and it fucked her up."

"Yeah, but they got her to an infirmary."

"Well," Gideon said. "We just better hope they have an infirmary here, or that suffocating on our own sick isn't as unpleasant as it sounds."

"Okay," Kiwi said, sitting in the captain's chair on the bridge. "You ready?"

"I think?" Noora said, sitting at her station, trying to interpret what was on her screen. "So this thing is facing aft?"

"Yup," Kiwi confirmed. "Best place I could fit it on the hull with the widest view."

"Okay, yeah, then. Good to go whenever you are."

"How's coolant flow?" Kiwi asked.

Noora checked her screen. "Coolant is flowing nicely, power diverted from engines to the rifle, we're in the green."

"Awesome. Got the *Sentinel* in your sights?" Kiwi asked.

"Boy, do I," Noora confirmed.

"All right then," Kiwi said. "Just like we talked about, aim for their right-starboard engine, and think of the rifle as a scalpel." She pulled out her phone and dialed Gideon's number.

It rang a few times before a familiar voice picked up. *"Hey,"* the voice said. *"I take it you're willing to play ball now?"*

"Hey, jackass," Kiwi answered dryly. "You're gonna put my boys on an escape pod, make sure their transponder is active so we can track them, and you're gonna send them up to coordinates $z + 500$ kilometers above your current position, where I'm currently sitting. If you don't do this right now, I'm gonna—"

"Sweetheart, look. I think you still don't understand the situation you're in."

Kiwi didn't hesitate, nor did she bother to hang up. "Fire," she said to Noora.

With surgical precision, Noora fired the Liminal across the weakest section of *The Sentinel's* right starboard engine, using it like a cutting beam. Within a few seconds, the engine was completely severed from the ship.

"What the fuck was that!" Jason's voice screamed over the phone, not at Kiwi, but at his crew.

"That was *me*, asshole!" Kiwi shouted, making sure he could hear her through all the alarms going off on his ship. "Now are you gonna give me my boys, or do you wanna lose another fucking engine!"

Noora whispered to Kiwi. "The Liminal's hot, we got maybe one more volley before it overheats."

Kiwi nodded. She knew her jury-rigged coolant system would only go so far. But Jason didn't know that.

"Hang on!" Jason begged. *"You just tore off one of my engines! I got a lot going on here!"*

"Well that sounds like a personal problem, jackass! Yes, or no, *now!*"

"Fine! Fine fine fine!"

"Good! You've got five minutes to launch them, or I take another engine. After that, they better be here in 10 minutes, or I take another engine. If I think for a *second* that you're trying to fuck with me, I'm splitting your ship in half. Got it?"

"Yeah, got it!" Jason shouted back before hanging up. He didn't have any time to waste.

Gideon and Dax, still bound and dehydrated in their interrogation room, suddenly heard a high-pitched pinging echoing through the bulkheads. It lasted less than 10 seconds, then stopped.

Followed by a couple explosions and unrelenting alarms. The room went dark and emergency lights came on.

"The fuck was that!" Gideon shouted over the alarms.

Dax laughed. "That was a 4-foot-11, 90-pound bottle of rage!" Dax shouted back. "You know her as *Kiwi!*"

"The hell did she do!"

"Something hilarious, I'm sure!"

A minute later, the door opened, and a panicked Jason, flanked by two guards, appeared. "Gettem up," he said to the guards. "Come on, gettem up, gettem up!"

The guards unbound Dax and Gideon, who were in no shape to resist.

"Everything all right?" Dax asked with some cheek. "I think I heard, like, a *pop* a minute ago."

"Gettem to escape pod 6 right now. Just throw them in and launch the goddamn thing."

"Oh," Gideon said. "Looks like Kiwi paid our ransom."

"That's one way of putting it," Jason said. He returned Gideon's phone to him by stuffing it into his jacket. "Get the fuck outta here."

The guards jogged the captives 50-feet down the corridor, throwing them into the escape pod, sealing it shut, and launching it immediately. Dax and Gideon didn't have a chance to even brace themselves. The launch slammed them into the steel floor, giving them a few more bumps and bruises.

Gideon realized Dax could hardly see with his two black eyes, and helped him into his harness first before getting into his own.

"They sure got us outta there quickly," Dax said. "Wonder what that was about."

"Well," Gideon said, pulling out his phone. "Let's find out." He called Kiwi, having a feeling she was nearby.

"Hey, retard!" she answered. *"Are you trying to test me? You barely launched that fucking pod on time!"*

Gideon and Dax couldn't help laughing. "Hey, Rosevine, it's me," Gideon said.

"Oh, shit, Gideon! I'm sorry, I thought fuckboy still had your phone. Noora, it's Gideon!"

"Yeah, no, it's me. I'm in the pod with Dax. I assume we're on our way to you?"

"Yup. You'll get to us in about, looks like 8 minutes. I told asshole he had 10, otherwise I'd cut his ship in half."

"With what? We don't have any weapons like that on the *Isle*."

"Well, um, maybe we do now," Kiwi said before changing the subject. *"You guys all right? You need anything when you dock?"*

"Yeah, I need you two not to freak out when you see our faces. See you in a few minutes."

"Holy fucking shet, Dax!" Noora exclaimed in her Finnish cadence. She rushed to Dax and got under his arm to help prop him up.

"I'm fine," Dax said, wincing as Noora put an arm around his ribs.

Kiwi was just entering the cargo bay, having stayed on the bridge to make sure the pod docked properly. "Hey, guys, how you—*holy shit what the fuck did they do to you!"*

"Here, let's sit you down," Noora said.

"No, it's um, yeah, you know what, that's a good idea," Dax said.

"You, too, Gideon!" Kiwi ordered.

"Jesus Christ, you both look like tenderized steak," Noora said, fetching a first aid kit.

Kiwi looked around for what she could grab, had an idea and said, "I'll be right back," and bolted out of the cargo bay.

"Just three black eyes and some bruised ribs," Gideon said. "Give us a few days, we'll be fine."

"You probably have concussions, too," Noora said, applying disinfectant to some gauze before cleaning Dax's face. "Especially you, Dax."

Kiwi shot back into the cargo bay, a jug of water in one hand, and a bottle of whiskey in the other. "Here," she said, handing the whiskey to Gideon. "Drink."

"Kiwi, they really need to hydrate," Noora said.

"No, no, it's fine," Dax said, wincing as Noora applied the antiseptic. "Whiskey first, then water."

Gideon took a long pull of the Twin Diesel bourbon before passing it to Dax, who took an even longer pull.

"So you wanna tell me about this new weapon we've got onboard?" Gideon asked.

"Well, it's not exactly new," Kiwi said.

"It's my Liminal," Noora said. "She rigged it for full-auto and attached it to the hull."

Dax scowled through his swollen black eyes. "How the fu—*how*?"

"Oh, I mean, you know," Kiwi said coyly. "I just, sort of, gave it a new receiver that could handle a high rate-of-fire, rigged a cooling jacket around the barrel, ran a line of coolant into it, and hooked the whole thing up to our engines."

Dax scoffed, then laughed. "Well shit, so *that's* what happened back there." He took another long pull of whiskey, then handed the bottle to Kiwi, who took a swig.

"Yeah, we kind of blew their right starboard engine clean off," she said.

"Dax, I need to get some real bandages for you, and maybe some ice packs, you just look terrible. And I'm staying with you tonight. I need to check you every few hours, make sure your brain doesn't have a concussion," Noora said.

Philly Cheesesteak entered the cargo bay through a vent, and came up to Gideon. *"Meh-r-r-r-reh,"* he greeted, rubbing against Gideon's leg.

"Hey there, Philly Phil, at least *someone's* giving me some attention," he joked.

Dax motioned his head at Kiwi, who gave him the whiskey back. He took another heavy pull.

"Dax, come on," Noora said. "You really need to get some water in you."

Dax ripped the bottle away, finally feeling the alcohol at work. "What I need is a goddamn vacation," he said. He looked towards where he thought Gideon was.

"Look, captain, I know you just spent several grueling days holed up in a comfortable hotel, but we've been at it a while. Can we just dock somewhere and get, like, a month of shore leave?"

"Yeah," Gideon nodded. "That sounds about right. I wanted to head to Earth anyway after this, since we're so close."

"I'm sorry, but, am I the only one worried we might be in trouble for shooting up another ship?" Noora asked.

"Don't worry, love," Gideon said. "They're 'independent contractors' just like us, doing legally questionable things, just like us. Jason and his crew aren't gonna alert anyone."

"And, I'm sorry, I have one more question," Noora said. "I know you hired me just for the Le Mons, but as long as my rifle is attached to this ship, I can't really go anywhere."

"Oh, looking to jump ship?" Gideon asked. "A pity. I thought you were fitting in nicely."

"Oh no, it's not that," Noora stated. "I actually think it would be, you know," she unconsciously glanced at Dax, and said, "I mean, if it's okay, I'd love to stick with you guys for a while."

"I was hoping you would," Gideon said, taking the whiskey bottle from Dax. "I've wanted a fourth person for a while, and there's no way we're finding someone else who can get along with Kiwi."

Kiwi nodded. "Yeah, I mean you're not wrong."

"Meh!" Philly Cheesesteak exclaimed.

"Yes, you're right," Gideon said, stroking Philly's chin. *"You're* the fourth, Noora's the fifth." He took a pull from the whiskey and offered Noora the bottle. "So what do you say?"

Noora accepted the bottle, reluctantly brought it to her mouth, and took a quick sip. She coughed and hacked as she swallowed the measure.

"Hey, to our new crewmate," Dax said, reaching for the bottle, but Noora snapped it away.

"No, Dax, you are done," she said.

Gideon took the bottle back from Noora, taking another swig. "Welcome aboard."

"Welcome, bestie," Kiwi said. "You get to celebrate by sleeping with Dax tonight," she teased.

"I am not, oh my gahd, I am not sleeping weth hem!" Noora protested, turning bright red as her Finnish accent came out. "I'm just, I'm gonna make sure your brain isn't fucked up, Dax. Come here. You need to lie down." She helped Dax stand, propping him up and leading him out of the cargo bay.

"Sleep well!" Kiwi teased again.

"Fuck you, Kiwi!" Noora shouted back.

Kiwi smiled, then looked at her captain. "How 'bout you, Sir Gideon? You gonna be okay? Cuz I'm *not* sleeping in your cabin to make sure you're all right."

"I'll be fine, Rosevine. Thanks for asking."

"Well you go get some sleep yourself. I'm gonna dump this pod back into space, then let the *Sentinel* know they can have it back if they can pick it up."

"Sounds good, love," Gideon said, standing up and heading for the exit.

"Philly Phil," Kiwi said. "Go sleep with uncle Gideon. Make sure to wake him up every few hours."

Philly Cheesesteak twitched his whiskers, then trotted after Gideon.

13. The Wisconsinite

Noora's rifle is a permanent part of the ship, Kiwi goes back to Wisconsin, and Philly Cheesesteak wrestles a chipmunk.

"Kiwi, what the fuck did you do?" Dax asked politely through his suit's shortwave.

"Jesus, Dax, your eyes still swollen shut?" Kiwi answered. *"I took a canon that was converted into a sniper rifle and converted it into a fully automatic angel of death and stuck it onto the ship. What do* think *I did?"*

"Did you tell Noora about this?" Dax asked, examining the Liminal's connections to the ship's outer hull.

"What do you mean? She fired the goddamn thing. Of course she knows."

"I mean did you tell her how she's not getting this rifle back?!" Dax asked. *"Look at this. There's no separating this cooling jacket from the barrel, I don't even know what you did with this hardware interface, you welded the whole thing to the ship, and whatever you did to connect this automatic receiver, I mean come on, there's no piecing this back to what it was."*

"I, I mean," Kiwi said, self-conscious. *"I mean I* thought *I could put it back together when I was doing it. It's the thought that counts, right?"*

Dax sighed in his suit. His eyes, still healing, itched like hell, and he was irritated he couldn't scratch them, more so than he was irritated at Kiwi. *"Well, look,"* he said. *"This thing is stuck to us. All we can really do is improve the coolant flow, but it's a permanent addition to the Isle."*

"Kinda like how Noora's a new addition to the Isle, you know?" Kiwi said.

Dax managed to smile in his suit. *"Well, open up the cargo bay hatch. I'm coming back in."*

"You don't wanna fix the coolant flow while you're out there?"

"Later," Dax said. *"I'm about to crack my helmet open, my eyes itch so fucking bad."*

"See? I knew you couldn't see!"

"So, um," Kiwi said awkwardly in the mess with Gideon, Dax, and Noora all looking at her. "Maybe we can't, uh, maybe like, your rifle is, like, permanently attached to the ship and we can't piece it back together to what it was." She hung her head low, feeling guilty.

"Oh, okay," Noora said, nonchalantly.

Kiwi looked up. "Is, is that okay?"

"I mean, it *was* an expensive rifle I won in competition, but honestly that thing was so cumbersome, and I could never really practically use it. Besides, what you did with it was brilliant. We saved Gideon and Dax, didn't we?"

"And actually," Gideon said. "I wanted to ask you, Noora, if we can keep it where it is. Obviously, we'd pay you for it, since it was yours."

Noora gave her stunned deer look, not knowing how to respond.

"Look," Gideon said. "Whatever Kiwi did, that thing does some serious damage, and given that the *Sentinel* has been chasing us around the solar system for a bit—"

"Not anymore, they're not," Kiwi said.

"I'd like to keep it as a sort of defensive policy," Gideon finished. "Don't know what we're gonna encounter in the future. I'd like to keep it on the ship, and since it was yours, we need to compensate you for it."

"Just take it out of my paycheck, Gideon," Kiwi said, still feeling bad. "I was the one that commandeered it."

"Tell you what," Gideon said. "You did the deed, and I want to keep it, so we'll take it out of both of our paychecks. Noora, how does that sound?"

"Oh, um, I mean," Noora said, not knowing how to respond.

Kiwi looked at her Finnish crewmate. "Just say yes, Noora."

"Yes?" Noora said.

"Excellent," Gideon said. "Might take us a few payouts to do it, but we'll do it. In the meantime, we're docking in Earth orbit in a couple days, so get together whatever you need for the next couple weeks, because the *Isle* is staying in orbit."

"Well who the hell's gonna take care of Philly Phil?" Kiwi asked.

On queue, Philly Cheesesteak entered the mess hall through an air vent.

Gideon shrugged his shoulders. "Any volunteers?"

"Meh!" Philly Cheesesteak snapped at Gideon.

"You can come with me, Philly Phil," Kiwi said. "We're going to Wisconsin, then we'll visit uncle Dax in East Texas, then we'll all go visit aunt Noora in Finland, then we'll pick up uncle Gideon wherever he's doing his next shady deal."

"Oh, is *that* what you're gonna do?" Dax asked, finally speaking up.

Kiwi gave him an assertive look. "Yes," she said.

Philly Cheesesteak jumped up on her lap and chirped. *"Br-r-r-r-eh."*

"So, Noora and I are dropping you off in Florida!" Gideon shouted over the dropship's turbulence. "Then we're jumping over to Europe from there."

"I fucking hate Florida, Gideon!" Kiwi shouted back.

"Too fucking bad! It's the easiest hub in North America to drop you two off at! Besides, you'll be there all of five minutes before you head off to whatever states you're from!"

"So rude!" Kiwi shouted at Dax. "Been working with him for how long and he still doesn't know where we're from!"

"Because we're all the same to these Europeans!" Dax shouted. "Cheeseburgers and cowboy hats!"

Noora smiled at Dax.

"Meh-r-r-rAO!" Philly Cheesesteak objected from his carrier.

The turbulence didn't last much longer, and they came to a powered descent into Cape Canaveral port.

"Bye, Kiwi. Bye Philly Phil. Take care, Dax," Noora said, as her compatriots grabbed their baggage, and Philly Cheesesteak's carrier, and exited the dropship.

"We're coming to see you, girl," Kiwi said to Noora. "I was serious. I'll text you, okay?"

"Okay!"

The dropship closed shut and immediately took off again, as Dax and Kiwi made their way along the tarmac to the transportation hub.

"You headed back home?" Kiwi asked.

"Yeah," Dax confirmed. "Once the family got wind I was coming back for a bit they planned a huge family get together."

"Oh fun! When's that happening? I wanna come down and meet your family!"

At first Dax was scared of the thought, then realized that if anything, Kiwi could save him from his own family. "Next weekend," he said as they reached the transportation hub, and they both started looking for their respective ways home.

"Oh that should be perfect!" Kiwi squealed. "I was planning on spending about a week on my grandparents' farm in Wisconsin anyway. I'll call you next Thursday!"

"Sounds good."

Kiwi dropped her metric ton of baggage and gave Dax a hug, to which he responded awkwardly, but as warmly as he was willing to manage. "Thanks, kid. You have fun."

"Try not to sulk the whole time, okay?" Kiwi said as she tried to re-sling her baggage, only for her small frame to topple off balance.

"Here, Jesus Christ, lemme help you with that," Dax said, picking up some of her baggage. "Where you headed?"

Kiwi checked her phone. "Uh, hub B5? I think? Wherever the line is that takes me to Chicago."

"That's B6. Here, gimme that crap, let's go. You grab Philly Cheesesteak."

"Mr-r-r-ao."

Several hours later, and three-and-a-half miles northeast of Lake Geneva, Wisconsin, Kiwi pulled up to her grandparents' farm in a rental.

Philly Cheesesteak was sick of his carrier, and demanded to be let out.

"Yes, yes, we're here, you little asshole," Kiwi said, opening the carrier, then opening the car door and letting Philly Cheesesteak out. "Don't go too far, okay? Stay close to the barn!"

"Breh-r-r-r-ryah!" Philly Phil acknowledged.

Kiwi got out of the car herself and pulled out her phone. She called her grandpa.

"Hey, you little shit!" he answered. *"Where the fuck are you?"*

"I'm *here* you old fuck, where the hell are *you?*"

"Oh, I see ya, I'm comin out."

Kiwi made her way up to the house. Her grandpa, stout and strong, and sharp as a tack, was out on the porch in a few seconds, coming down the stairs to greet her. "Hey you!"

"Grandpa bear!" Kiwi shouted, running up to him and hugging him tightly.

He returned the hug and tried to give her a big kiss on the head, only to get a mess of raven black hair in his mouth. "Blah! Get this shit outta my mouth! How the hell ya been? More importantly, what did you bring me?"

"Well let's see," Kiwi said. "I've committed corporate theft around Uranus, got kidnapped on Titan, overdosed myself just to spite my captors, sabotaged some rally car race on Mars, slept with a racer from Finland, ripped an engine off a starship using a sniper rifle I repurposed into an automatic bringer of death, oh and I made a new friend who's actually a woman!"

Grandpa, mouth wide open, stared in disbelief. "There's no fucking way you made friends with a woman."

"I know, right!" Kiwi said. "Oh, and I got you a case of Twin Diesel bourbon. I drank most of it, but, uh—"

"Holy shit!" Grandpa exclaimed. "That's *impossible* to get here! You know how hard I've been trying to get just a bottle of that?"

"Well, I got, you know, part of a case for us to drink together," Kiwi said. "Where's grandma, by the way?"

"Oh she's insi—, hey *sweetie!*" Grandpa shouted into the house. "Get your sexy ass out here! Kiwi's here!" He looked to Kiwi. "You must be starving. Look at you, you're *still* too skinny!"

At that moment, Grandma came outside. A whip handle to Grandpa's stout strength. "Oh my goodness, *Kiwi!*" she exclaimed, going up to Kiwi and giving her a hug. "Oh my goodness, I'm so happy you're here."

"Love you, Grandma bear," Kiwi said.

Grandma looked at Grandpa. "We need to start cooking, now."

"You mean *I* need to start cooking," Grandpa said.

"That's what I said," Grandma said.

"You guys mind if we grill outside?" Kiwi asked. "Being back in Earth gravity, breathing Earth air, I hadn't realized how much I missed being outside."

"Of course not!" Grandpa proclaimed. "Lemme get the grill fired up, I'll be out back."

"He can't wait to show off his new grill," Grandma said.

"Oh, by the way, I've got Philly Cheesesteak with me. I let him out and told him to go hang out by the barn, if that's okay?"

"Oh that's fine dear. Is that your car? Here, lemme help with your stuff."

"Jesus Christ," Kiwi said, stomach full and brain tipsy. "You're almost as good of a cook as my ship's engineer."

"Hey, fuck you, Kiwi," Grandpa said, helping himself to more of the Twin Diesel bourbon. "You're lucky you brought this stuff, otherwise you'd be sleeping out in the barn."

"Oh now watch your mouth, Richard," Grandma said. "Kiwi was kidding."

"No I wasn't," Kiwi said, pouring herself more bourbon as well. "And actually, is it cool if I sleep out in the barn?"

"Well I've got your bed all made up for you upstairs if you'd like, but yeah we can set up the cot in the barn, and really do you both need your own bottle of whiskey?" Grandma said.

"Yes!" Kiwi and Grandpa answered at the same time. "Come on, sweetie, at least try a sip and tell me how much you hate it," Grandpa said, holding out a bottle of the Twin Diesel.

Grandma rolled her eyes, but held out her glass. Grandpa poured her a splash. She sniffed it skeptically, then drained it. Her face scrimped up, then relaxed. She smacked her lips and said, "Huh," then held her glass out for another pour.

"Holy shit, Kiwi, I think she likes it!" Grandpa said, pouring a measure.

"It's good stuff!" Kiwi said.

"Tastes even sweeter knowing you flew it a billion miles to get it to us," Grandpa said, holding up the bottle as if to say 'cheers'.

Kiwi held up her own glass, then drained it, then coughed. "Whew, damn, it's smooth!"

"Have you had enough to eat, dear?" Grandma asked.

"Yes, Grandma bear, holy shit, do you see my bulging stomach?"

Grandma looked at Kiwi's stomach. "No."

"Well trust me, I'm good," Kiwi said.

"You know you've both been drinking a lot, lemme get you some water," Grandma said, getting up and heading into the house.

Kiwi poured herself another measure, then held up her glass and clanked it with Grandpa's. "It's great to be here and see you guys," she said.

Grandpa's smile was warm. "It's great seeing you, too, kid," he said, before changing his tone. "You know, you haven't asked about your mom."

Kiwi sighed, and tried to act like a dark cloud wasn't suddenly hanging over her head. "Not to sound like a bitch, but what's to ask?"

Grandpa scoffed a laugh, shrugged, and said, "Nothing, I guess."

Kiwi drained her glass, trying not to show her wave of anger. "Well, where is she?"

"Chicago," Grandpa said, taking a sip from his glass.

"Still?" Kiwi asked.

"Yup. So you're right. Nothing's changed, and she's still, you know—"

"A drug-addled psycho?" Kiwi asked rhetorically.

Grandpa shrugged again, hesitant to say the truth about his own daughter.

Kiwi nodded. "Thanks. I'm sorry, it's just—"

"No, don't be sorry," Grandpa said. "I know what she put you through."

Grandma came back out with two ice waters. Kiwi and Grandpa both readjusted their demeanors. "Here you both go, now drink up," she said.

"Thank you, Grandma."

"Thank you, sweetie."

"Hey," Kiwi said, switching the subject. "Is my whip still hung up in the barn?"

"Oh of course it is," Grandpa said. "You may need to dust it off, but we'd never get rid of it."

"Also, you have any equipment that needs fixing?" Kiwi asked.

"Oh yeah," Grandpa said. "One of the tractors is only firing on two cylinders instead of all four. I was gonna get to it sometime, but help yourself."

"Oh now don't take advantage of her like that," Grandma said.

"What do you mean take advantage?" Grandpa asked. "That's escapism for her!"

"He's right, Grandma," Kiwi said, standing up. "Look, I'm gonna set up in the barn. All this traveling and all this food and all this booze is making me tired."

"Oh, well let me get you the cot, dear," Grandma said.

"No, I got it, you sit down," Kiwi said. "Great dinner, Grandpa bear. Seriously, you're almost as good as my ship's chef."

Grandpa laughed and held up his glass of Twin Diesel bourbon. "Glad to have you with us, kiddo."

Kiwi writhed to her industrial rock, in the barn, screaming with the lyrics while she mended her Grandpa's diesel tractor.

"Cuuuuuuuzz I got a fuckin pistol right on my hip, and I got it backed up, yeah, with two clips!"

"Kiwi," Grandpa shouted, trying to get her attention.

"Just try and test me, bitch, cuz I'll shoot that shit, right in yo fuckin face cuz I'm a mutha-fuckin bitch!"

"Kiwi!" Grandpa shouted again.

"Oh! Hey!" Kiwi shouted back, turning the music down.

"How's it looking?" Grandpa asked, indicating his tractor.

"Oh, yeah, no, the injectors are just off on these two cylinders. I'm gonna test it in a second, but should be good to go when I'm done."

"Oh that's great!" Grandpa said. "By the way, where's that cat you brought?"

"Last I saw him he was wrestling with a chipmunk just outside the barn. Think he made a new friend."

"Well lemme know if you need anything," Grandpa said.

"I don't need *anything*. You need *me* to fix all your shit!" Kiwi said.

Grandpa smiled.

Kiwi woke up in the barn, only slightly hungover. She grabbed the glass of water by her cot and chugged it, trying to remember how many days she'd been back in Wisconsin.

Philly Cheesesteak, already mildly awake, greeted her with, *"Meo-r-r-reh."*

"Hey, little Philly bear bear," Kiwi said, patting his head. She got up and stretched, thinking about the leather whip she'd gotten as a kid, that her grandparents still kept hung up in the barn, then thought it would be a great way to warm herself up from the early autumn night.

She climbed down the ladder to the barn floor.

"Meh-r-r-r-r-reh!" Philly Cheesesteak said.

"You got up there," Kiwi pointed out. "You can figure out how to get down!"

"Mreh!" Philly Cheesesteak protested.

Kiwi grabbed her coiled whip, hung on an iron fitting. She grabbed a rusted steel target as well, planning on smacking the thing with a bunch of rage, only for her phone to ring.

It was Dax.

"Jesus Christ, Dax, the fuck you calling me at this time in the morning?" she asked.

"The fuck you mean? It's 10:30!" Dax answered.

Kiwi looked at the time on her phone. "Yeah, the fuck you calling me so early?"

"Well, look," Dax said. *"The sooner you can get your ass to East Texas, the better."*

Kiwi smiled. "Dax? Are you asking me to come save you?"

"Yes, I am," Dax admitted. *"Just don't ever tell anyone I said that."*

"Well, I'll see how soon I can get there. I'll text you," she said, and hung up.

Philly Cheesesteak had managed to vault himself down to the ground.

"Well look, you little shithead," Kiwi said to him. "I'm heading off to save Uncle Dax. You stay here. Enjoy the countryside. I'll come back to get you."

Philly Cheesesteak blinked his eyes slowly in agreement.

14. The East Texan

Dax hates chardonnay, Dax hates social gatherings, and Dax hates his former boss.

"You from Marshall?" the driver asked, recognizing Dax's accent.

"Yeah," Dax answered, hoping the conversation wouldn't continue.

"Visiting family?"

"Yeah," Dax said, pulling out his phone. "Sorry, I gotta make a call." He rang up his mother.

"Hey, Dax," she answered, trying to talk over the commotion of conversations and laughter in the background.

Dax was overstimulated already. "Hey, I'm like three minutes away. Just wanted you to know. Is the whole family there already?"

"Oh no, just your dad, your brother and your sister and their families, HEY EVERYONE DAX IS ALMOST HERE!"

Dax did the arithmetic. That was at least 11 people already. He wondered how much patience he'd have left by the end of the week. "See ya in a minute." He hung up and then said to the driver, "You can let me out here."

"We're still several blocks away," the driver said.

"I know, now pull over and let me out," Dax said.

"Okay, no problem, here we are, and thank you and you have a great rest of your day," the driver said.

"Thank you, you too," Dax said, feeling bad for having been so terse. He got out of the car, mopped his long, wavy hair behind his head and tied it back, and slung his duffle bag over his shoulder.

He was gonna need a few blocks of quiet to himself before his family swarmed him.

"Dax!"

"Daaax!"

"Hey, Dax!"

"Hi, Dax!"

"Hey, Uncle Dax!"

Dax was genuinely happy to see his immediate family, then mentally swore at himself; he'd forgotten to bring something for everyone.

But everyone was kind. Much kinder than usual, in fact, as they had been every time they'd seen him over the last three years. He wished they would treat him normally, but they were just trying to be kind.

After navigating the standard "how are you" and "how've you been" from everyone, and returning the favor, he pulled his tall, lanky mom aside and asked, "Hey, do you have a bottle of wine? I'm sorry, I forgot to pick one up on the way here. Wanted to, you know, go do my thing."

"Oh of course, dear," his mom answered discreetly, knowing what it was for. "Chardonnay, right?"

"Yeah, chardonnay if you got it."

His mom grabbed a cold bottle of chardonnay from the fridge and handed it to him, saying, "I take it you haven't, you know, found anyone? I mean it's been three years."

"Three years, four months, nine days," Dax said, accepting the bottle. "Not that I'm counting."

"She would've wanted you to move on, Dax. I'm just saying."

"I know what she would've wanted better than anyone else," Dax said, irritated at her comment, but keeping his tone respectful. "I'll be back in an hour or so. Tell dad to fire up the smoker in half an hour. I'll grill us up some steaks or something when I get back."

He stopped in the garage to grab a folding chair, then made his way to the cemetery half a mile away.

Late afternoon on a weekday, Dax was the only one in the cemetery, which he preferred. Not that a crowd of people would make him self conscious, he just preferred having a drink with his wife alone.

He found her headstone, said, "Hey," unfolded the chair, sat down, and ripped the cap off the chardonnay. "Still cold, well, *mostly* still cold," he said, pouring a few ounces over her name, then taking a long pull himself.

He sat back and conversed with her like he always did, imagining what she would say, and responding as he normally would.

Thanks for the chardonnay.

"You're goddamn right. I'd rather be drinking wood alcohol."

[smiles] How many times have you said that joke?
"Not a joke."

[smiles again] What brings you back to town?

"Shore leave. Gideon and I got the shit kicked out of us on Mars. Told him I needed a month of vacation. Getting about two weeks."

Jesus Christ, Dax, what happened?

"Oh," Dax waved it off, taking another pull of chardonnay. "Long story. Let's just say we committed some corporate robbery, and this one dude has had a hard-on for us since. I think he got hired by the company we stole from. Caught up to me and Gideon, but Kiwi saved our asses." He took another drink.

Don't drink all of that yourself! You don't even like it!

"You're right, I'm sorry," he said, pouring a few more ounces on her headstone.

How's Kiwi doing, by the way? Still driving you crazy?

"She finds new ways everyday," Dax said, taking a sip. "But no, she's good. She's up in Wisconsin visiting her grandparents."

Her grandparents, huh?

"Yeah, sad story, her dad died before she was born, and her mom is a deadbeat psycho. Her grandparents raised her, but they seem like good people." He poured more chardonnay on her headstone.

You probably haven't met anyone now that you're traveling around space, have you?

Dax rolled his eyes. "I've been back in town for less than an hour, and you're already the second person to ask me that."

Because you should at least have tried to date someone by now, Dax.

Dax held up his hands. "Can I just do things at my own pace? Like, can I just do that?"

You haven't even answered the question.

Dax knew he couldn't hide anything from her. "So, we have a new crew member."

So you have *met someone! Tell me about her!*

Dax felt awkward, so took another drink. "There's not much to tell. We picked her up on Titan what, a few months ago. She's Finnish. She's a sniper. She's cut like a slab of marble."

Okay, so she's hot.

"Yeah," Dax sighed, feeling uncomfortable about the subject. "Yeah. She's cool, too. I don't know."

Have you guys been hooking up?

"No, Jesus Christ, besides I've got at least 10 years on her, if not more," Dax exclaimed. "I'm sorry, can we talk about something else?"

Of course, I'm sorry.

"No, no, *I'm* sorry," he said, pouring out more chardonnay.

How long are you here for?

"Dunno. My parents organized a family get-together. How long do you think I'll be able to stand that?"

[laughs] They're not trying to torture you, you know.

"I know," Dax said, taking one last pull of chardonnay before draining the rest of it over her headstone. "Look, I gotta get back. Told everyone I'd cook for them, and I gotta stop at the store on the way." He leaned the empty chardonnay bottle against her headstone.

Thanks for always stopping by, Dax.

"I'll be back tomorrow. I'll tell you all about how Gideon and I got kidnapped and beaten up."

Fun! You can leave the chair, by the way. No one's gonna take it.

"You got it. Good seeing you, sweetie."

Good seeing you, dear.

"I had 20 chairs in the garage!" Dax's father exclaimed. "I know, because I counted them and was like, 'well shit I've only got 20 chairs that's not nearly enough for everyone'! Now there's only 19!"

"19's not enough? What'd you do, invite the whole Spanish Armada?" Dax asked, referring to his father's side of the family.

"Yes! And the French Bourgeois," his father said, referring to his mother's side of the family.

Dax did a quick mental tally of how many people that was, and lost count after 60.

"Anyway," his father said, in his boundless energy. "I'm gonna run to the store. Grab some more chairs. You need anything, head chef?"

"Yeah," Dax said, realizing he'd gravely underestimated how many people were showing up, and thereby how much stress it was going to cause him. "I need, like, all the liquor you can buy, and like any and all meat they have at—you know what just lemme come with you."

"Okay, I'm gonna run to the restroom first, be right out."

Dax took a deep breath. He'd always waged a pitched mental battle between needing to be social with his massive family, and needing to be left the hell alone. Add to that, everyone had tried to be awkwardly nice to him since Rochelle had died, and he nearly had a panic attack at the prospect of the several dozen of people that were about to swarm his parents' place.

He decided to skip immediately to his last resort.

He called Kiwi.

"Jesus Christ, Dax, the fuck you calling me at this time in the morning?" she answered.

"The fuck you mean? It's 10:30!" Dax said.

"Yeah, the fuck you calling me so early?"

"Well, look," Dax said. "The sooner you can get your ass to East Texas, the better."

"Dax?" Kiwi asked skeptically. *"Are you asking me to come save you?"*

"Yes, I am," Dax admitted. "Just don't ever tell anyone I said that."

"Well, I'll see how soon I can get there. I'll text you," Kiwi said, and hung up.

Dax sighed in relief. Whatever chaos Kiwi might bring would be preferable to the social pain he was about to be subjected to.

His father returned from the restroom. "Ready?"

"Let's go."

Dax was grateful his family put him in charge of the grill when he was home. Without something to focus on, he'd go insane.

"Uncle Dax, do you, like, do you like travel around in space?"

"I do, and the lifestyle suits me."

"Yo Dax, I hear you make good money out in space."

"Great money. Turns out not a lot of people enjoy just how vast and empty space is."

"Hey Dax, how's that chicken looking?"

"Might be the best chicken I've ever made."

"Hey, Dax, how ya been since, you know…?"

"I've been fine."

His ability to tolerate his own family surprised himself. The bottle of bourbon he kept by the grill helped, but he had his limits.

As the cacophony of endless conversations made him approach his limit, he heard the angel of chaos call out his name, and suddenly he knew he was going to be fine.

"Daaaaaaax!" Kiwi shouted from across the yard. "Oh my god, come here!" She ran across the yard and threw herself into his side.

"Holy shit, Rosevine," he said, throwing an arm around her. "And not a moment too soon."

"Is this all your family?" she asked. "Jesus Christ, I didn't know you had such a huge family! And you *hate* people!"

"Tell me about it. Bourbon?"

"Oh my god, yes."

Dax poured her a massive measure.

Kiwi drained most of it. "*Dahhh*," she exclaimed. "All right, so who's who? I wanna meet your parents, oh my god!"

"Well, they're, uh," Dax said before being interrupted by his brother.

"Hey man," his brother said. "Just wanted you to know that, uh, Michael is here."

Dax's tone suddenly shifted. "The *fuck* you mean, *Michael is here?*"

"It's just that, you know, he's seeing Marie," his brother responded.

"Marie. Which cousin is that?" Dax asked.

His brother shrugged. "I'm just tellin you he's here, man."

"Dax, you wanna introduce me to this gentleman?" Kiwi demanded.

"Yeah, this is, uh, this is my brother, Allain. Allain, this is Kiwi, one of my crewmates," Dax said.

"Allain!" Kiwi squealed. "Is that French?"

"Yeah, um," Allain said. "Yeah it is, how'd you know?"

Kiwi walked off with Allain, while Dax tried to channel his rage. He pretended to pay attention to the grill, but ended up looking around the yard for Michael.

He found him quickly, making eye contact. Michael, skinny fat and with the spine of a wet noodle, lifted his head in acknowledgement. Dax looked back at the grill, gritting his teeth.

Before he knew it, Michael had made his way to him.

"Hey, Dax, it's been a while. How have you, um, how've you been?" Michael asked.

Dax grabbed the bottle of bourbon, stared at Michael while taking a long pull, ripped the bottle away, and spat a clot of saliva towards Michael's shoes.

"I've been *fucking* great, Michael," he said loudly. "How the *fuck* have *you* been?"

Everyone surrounding the grill dropped their conversations and stared. A ripple effect went through the backyard.

"I, um," Michael said, "I mean, I've been fine."

Dax, angry enough to not care, threw an arm around Michael and announced to the entire gathering: "Hey, everyone, just want you to know that Michael is *fucking* fine!"

"I just," Michael protested. "I mean, Dax, come on."

Dax kept up his shouting. "This *sucking, fucking* piece of shit, who tried to get me fired when my fucking wife died just wants all of you to know that he's *fucking* fine!"

The entire yard was now silent. Even Kiwi was staring at him, jaw agape.

"Was there anything else you wanted to *say*, Michael!" Dax screamed. "You fucking dick-sucking pig?"

Michael was silent, as was the rest of the yard.

"Wait," Kiwi said to Allain. "Wait what? Dax is married? *Was* married?"

"Didn't think so!" Dax screamed into Michael's face. He grabbed the bottle of bourbon and headed off. No one tried to stop him.

The rest of the yard was silent, except for Kiwi, who followed him. "Wait! Jesus Christ, I'm so confused! Dax, hang on, where are you going?"

"Hey, come on, where are you going?" Kiwi asked, walking beside him.

"Just, just walk with me, okay?" he said, handing her the bottle of bourbon.

Kiwi took a swig, then handed it back. "Jesus, I knew you hated people, but not like *that*."

"It's just, it's a long story," Dax said.

"And you're *married*? Or *were* married?" Kiwi said.

"Well you're about to find out," Dax said, taking a pull from the bourbon. He led her to the cemetery, up to his wife's headstone.

Kiwi looked at the headstone, saw the name, and the dates, and several bottles of chardonnay leaned against it, and said, "Oh my god, no, Jesus Christ, Dax, I just, I had no idea."

Dax poured out some bourbon on Rochelle's name. "Sorry, I know you're not a fan of bourbon," he said.

Kiwi latched on with a hug. "Dax, I'm so, I mean, like, how long were you married?"

"14 years," he said.

"Like, do you have kids, or anything?" Kiwi asked.

"No," Dax said. "We, uh, anyway, no."

"I'm so sorry," Kiwi said.

Dax wrapped an arm around her, grateful she was with him. "Thanks for coming," he said.

"Is this why you're not banging Noora?" Kiwi asked.

Dax rolled his eyes and let go. "Jesus *fucking* Christ, Kiwi!"

"Well what the hell is wrong with you, Dax? Like, look," Kiwi counted the years from Rochelle's date of death. "It's been over three years! And you wonder why I'm always trying to get you laid!"

"Can I not take things at my own *fucking* pace?" Dax asked rhetorically. He looked at Rochelle's headstone. "Can I not!"

Kiwi snatched the bottle of bourbon from him and took a hefty pull.

"Gimme that," Dax said, snatching it back and taking his own pull. He looked at Rochelle's headstone again, and laughed. "Yeah, I figured you would," he said.

Kiwi scowled. "Who the hell you talking to?"

"It's, uh, it's nothing," Dax said. "Rochelle would've liked you."

Kiwi lifted a skeptical eyebrow. "Even though I drive you crazy?"

"*Especially* because you drive me crazy."

Kiwi laughed, and gave him another hug, before saying, "Hey, you need to get outta here? I told Noora I'd meet up with her. In Finland, of all places."

"Well, that *is* where she's from," Dax pointed out.

"Yeah," Kiwi said, dialing Noora's number. "But I've never been to Finland. You?"

Dax shook his head. "Couldn't point to it on a map."

"Hey, Kiwi!" Noora answered.

"Noor-r-ra!" Kiwi exclaimed in her best Finnish impression. "I told you I was gonna come see you!"

"Of course! Are you still in Wisconsin?"

"No, I'm in, where are we again? I'm in Marshall, Texas, and I need to get Dax the hell outta here. Cool if he comes too?"

"Oh, um, yeah, *of—of course!"* Noora said, pleasantly surprised.

"She's excited to see you," Kiwi quietly said to Dax. "So look, don't know when we'll get there, but I'll keep you posted, okay? You're in Helsinki, right?"

"Yes! Well, just outside, actually. But yeah, just get to Helsinki and I can pick you guys up."

Kiwi hung up, grabbed the bourbon, took a swig and said, "So, when can you be ready to go?"

Dax took the bourbon back. "Figure two minutes to pack up my stuff, then about two hours to say goodbye to everyone, though don't know if they want me around after my spectacle back there." He poured a measure onto Rochelle's headstone, saying, "I'll see you," under his breath.

Dax grabbed the folding chair that had been sitting there all week, and they made their way back towards the house.

"That cocksucker really tried to fire you?"

"Yup," Dax said.

"How? Why? All you do is work."

"Let's just say I wanted more than five days of bereavement after Rochelle died, and he was not amenable to the idea. And I may have threatened to knock his teeth out when he wouldn't let me take more time off. My biggest regret is I didn't do it. And now turns out he's seeing one of my 30 cousins."

"Well," Kiwi said. "I mean there's still time to knock his teeth out."

Dax finally managed a smile. "Thanks for coming to get me."

15. The Finn

Noora has reverse culture shock, Noora and her sister are anime and cosplay fans, and Kiwi invites Finland's only celebrity to Noora's parents' house.

Noora had a problem.

She was back in her home country, in her hometown for the first time in 11 months, surrounded by familiar sights, sounds, and customs.

She was speaking her native language, eating the foods she'd grown up with, even stuffing herself with a Karelian pastry when her stomach allowed.

She was with her parents, who loved her, and her younger sister, with whom she gossiped.

And she felt out of place, unable to determine why.

Feeling like a foreigner in her own country, which she'd never been away from for more than two weeks, left a strange anxiety in her.

But she kept it to herself.

"So," her parents asked her over a dinner of smoked salmon and rye bread. "What are you going to do now that you're back?" They'd even broken out a special bottle of mead to celebrate their eldest daughter's return.

"Well," Noora said, awkwardly. "I'm actually heading back out in, like, a couple weeks."

"You mean," her father asked, pointing up, "going back out into space?"

Noora pinched her lips and nodded.

"Where are you going?" her mother asked.

"I, um, I don't know. Not yet, anyway."

"Why do you want to go back out into space?" her father asked.

"I just," Noora shrugged, hearing the disappointment in his tone. "I mean, the captain, Gideon, he asked me to join them, and I've already said yes."

"But why do you *want* to go back out into space?" her mother asked. "You went out to, where was it, Titan? To that space station? For that sharpshooter competition. I mean, I understand wanting to get off-world once for fun, but getting there took most of what you had saved up. You've got everything else you need here."

Realizing her parents, while they loved her, had a unique talent for making her feel guilty, Noora decided to switch the subject.

She looked to her younger sister. "So tell me, you've got *Euro-Con* coming up. Who are you going as?"

"Oh!" Niina said through a mouthful of smoked salmon and rye bread. "You know Dizzy from *Tenjou Rayden*?"

"Oh my god I love Dizzy from Tenjou!" Noora squealed. "You have to show me your costume after dinner!"

"It's still not done," Niina said. "I mean I've got a lot more to go."

"Well that's why you have to let me help you!" Noora said.

"Really, I don't understand why you spend all that time and money on those silly cosplays of those strange Japanese characters," their mother said.

"Because it's fun, mom!" Noora said, more for herself than for her sister. She turned back to Niina. "Come on, you have to show me!"

"That is *sooo* cute, oh my god!" Noora exclaimed.

"But there's so much I have to do!" Niina complained. "I don't know how to do it all!"

"I mean, the whole French maid look is solid, you just need the gold lace, the golden gauntlets, the rose ruffles, oh and how are you gonna do the leg and neck tattoos?" Noora asked.

"I have no idea."

Noora smiled. "You know, I never realized it, but Dizzy reminds me of one of my crewmates. Like, her attitude, her look, it's hilarious."

"Is that Kiwi?"

"Oh of course, you would love her. She actually said she wanted to visit me sometime while we're back on Earth, so you might get to meet her." Noora helped herself to Niina's cosplay supplies. "Here, let me do, like, a stencil design for the tattoos. Then you can just paint it on easily."

"I can't believe you're really going back out into space," Niina said. "Mom and dad do *not* like that idea. I mean they didn't like it when you flew out to Saturn!"

"I know," Noora said. "But, like, I didn't tell them this, but I've already more than made back the money I spent getting out there."

"Oo! Doing what?" Niina asked. "And why'd they hire you, anyway?"

Noora pretended to concentrate on the stencil design, trying to think how she could avoid explaining what she'd been up to, then realized she couldn't keep anything from her sister.

"Okay," she finally said, putting the stencil design down. "So, I won that competition on Titan, right? Well, I won this huge fucking rifle, and I mean it's *big*. It's basically a ship cannon turned into a rifle. Can fire a .22 at 5% the speed of light."

Niina sat down and listened.

"So, like," Noora continues. "Word gets around the station that I won, and all these guys start asking me for shooting lessons, but then they really wanna shoot that rifle, so they'd pay me to take a shuttle out, and go plink rocks in Saturn's rings. I made some good money, but it got repetitive after a while, and plus too many guys were trying to hit on me."

"And then one day," Noora said. "I see this ad on the station's job board. Some independent contractor looking for a sharpshooter. So I go interview with them, and that's where I met Gideon, Dax, and Kiwi. *Oh*, and Philly Cheesesteak?"

"Philly Cheesesteak?" Niina asked.

"He's their kitty cat. He's silver and black, but his underbelly is all white, he's super cute."

"You guys have a cat in space?" Niina asked.

"Yeah, we sometimes get stowaway rats, so helps to have a cat on board. Anyway, they hire me, and get this," Noora said, her voice suddenly turning to a whisper. "You know Le Mons, right?"

"Of course!" Niina said. "Fucking Raikkonen didn't even place this year, though."

"So get this," Noora said, her voice still quiet. "They hired me to shoot out Raikkonen's tires."

Niina's jaw went agape. "They hired you to shoot out—!"

"Shhhhhh!" Noora exclaimed. "But like, I never got a clean shot. I never actually did it. But get this, fucking *Kiwi* meets Raikkonen by accident, sleeps with him and gets him hungover the whole race, *and she didn't even know it was him!*"

"What!" Niina exclaimed. "How could she *not* know who Raikkonen is!"

"She's American and she doesn't care about rally car racing," Noora said. "So that's why Raikkonen didn't even place. And after that, fucking Gideon and Dax get *kidnapped.*"

"What! By *who?*" Niina asked.

"I don't know! Some guy, I think his name is Jason? He'd been chasing them for a while. So Kiwi's like, 'Noora, we need to save Dax and Gideon—"

"Wait, why had he been chasing them?" Niina asked.

Noora shook her head, trying to remember what Kiwi had said. "I think because of something they had stolen? I don't know. So anyway, Kiwi and I are on the ship, and that rifle I won, she turns it into this fully automatic fucking blast cannon, welds it to the outside of the ship, opens up a comm with them, and says 'return Dax and Gideon now or we shoot,' and of course they didn't listen, so get this, *oh my god*, get this, Kiwi has me operate the rifle, and I blew one of their engines clean off!"

Niina didn't know what to say.

"So they start freaking out, and Kiwi's like, 'I'll cut your ship in half if you don't return them now,' so they returned them. And oh my god, they were both beat up, Dax especially, but I guess he kicked the shit out of a number of their guys, and that's when they decided they needed a vacation, so we're back here. But Gideon was like, 'hey, you really fit in with the crew, and we stole your rifle so we gotta pay you for that, why don't you stay on?' and I was like, yeah why not."

Niina shook her head in shock. "Jesus Christ, Noora. Who *are* these people?"

"Well Gideon's the captain, he owns the *Isle of Skye*. And I told you about Kiwi. Just imagine Dizzy, but turned up to 11. And there's Dax. Oh my god, Dax is great.

He's, like, the ship's engineer, but he's also the one that cooks, and he's such a great chef, my god I get all the ribeyes I want, and he's like really smart, and Jesus Christ his arms, and he's like dark and brooding and pissed off all the time but he's super funny and just doesn't give a fuck…"

Niina raised an eyebrow.

Noora noticed it, then face-palmed herself. "Okay, okay, *yes*, I like him, I just, I don't know."

"And?" Niina asked.

"And, I don't know, he's just like, he's got this long, wavy hair, he's half Spanish so he's got that Mediterranean look, but he's also from East Texas, so he's got this thick, like, southern American accent, and, like, I don't know."

"Have you two, been, you know?"

"Oh my god no!" Noora exclaimed. "I'm too shy, I don't know how to approach guys."

"Is he the reason you're going back out with them?" Niina asked.

Noora took a second to think. "Honestly, no," she said. "He's great, I like him, but it's, I mean, it's something else."

Niina yawned. Noora followed suit. "I'm sorry, I'm keeping you up with all my stories," she said.

"No!" Niina insisted. "It's fun! Let's keep talking tomorrow."

"Of course!"

Noora went to her bedroom, thinking about everything she had confided in her sister, realizing what her problem was.

After almost a year off-world, traveling around the solar system, and the last few months with the *Isle of Skye* crew, the comforts and familiarity of her home country lacked the one thing she needed.

Adventure.

Noora went through what her rituals used to be over the next week, but found them foreign.

She went to her local gym, but missed the convenience of the workout room on the *Isle*.

She enjoyed her local cuisine, but missed Dax's cooking.

She interacted with everyone in their shared, Finnish way, but missed the Americanism of Kiwi and Dax, and the dry humor of her Scottish captain.

It's when the reverse culture shock was at its worst that she got the call from Kiwi.

"Hey, Kiwi!" Noora answered.

"Noor-r-ra!" Kiwi exclaimed in her best Finnish impression. *"I told you I was gonna come see you!"*

"Of course! Are you still in Wisconsin?"

"No, I'm in, where are we again? I'm in Marshall, Texas, and I need to get Dax the hell outta here. Cool if he comes too?"

"Oh, um, yeah, of—of course!" Noora said, pleasantly surprised.

Kiwi said something quietly to someone else, then said, *"So look, don't know when we'll get there, but I'll keep you posted, okay? You're in Helsinki, right?"*

"Yes! Well, just outside, actually. But yeah, just get to Helsinki and I can pick you guys up."

They hung up, and Noora started freaking out.

She ran to her sister's room. Niina was watching *Tenjou Rayden* in Japanese, with Finnish subtitles.

"Oh my god!" Noora exclaimed.

"Oh my god, *what?"* Niina said back.

"Kiwi's coming!" Noora shouted. "With Dax! *Oh my fucking god she's coming with Dax what the fuck do I do!"*

The sense of adventure was back.

"Okay," Noora said. "We've got the pork, the salmon, some Karelian pastries, plenty of bread, and what do we have for alcohol?"

"Oh," Noora's mother said. "We've got a bottle of wine. *Oh*, and a bottle of mead. Do you think Americans like mead?"

Noora's jaw was on the floor. "That's *it*?" she asked.

Her mother nodded.

"Okay, I need to run to the store," Noora said.

"For what?" her mother asked.

"I just, look," Noora said. "I don't know if it's an American thing or what, but these two both drink enough to kill an elephant. We need all the beer and whiskey we can get."

"Thank you so much for having us!" Kiwi exclaimed, popping her second beer.

"Yeah," Dax said. "What she said, but respectfully."

Noora, sitting next to Dax, giggled.

Kiwi scowled. "*I was* respectful, jackass."

"Were you, though?" Dax asked.

"Well, it's wonderful to have you here," Noora's mother said in English. "And it's great to meet Noora's co-workers."

"Hey, to co-workers," Kiwi said, raising her can of beer.

"To co-workers," Dax said, raising his glass of whiskey.

"To co-workers," Noora said, raising her glass of mead.

"What's that you're drinking?" Dax asked Noora.

"Oh, it's mead, would you like some?"

"Yeah, may I?" Dax said, draining his whiskey in one gulp and offering up his glass.

Noora smiled, delicately pouring him a measure.

Niina, her sister, watched the two of them closely.

Dax swirled the mead, enjoying its fragrance. He contemplated it, and sipped it like a wine connoisseur.

Noora's whole family watched for his reaction.

"This is wonderful," he said. He looked at Noora's parents. "I've never had mead before. Thank you."

Kiwi gave Dax a look. "Are you all right?" she asked.

"What do you mean?" Dax asked back.

"You're, like, polite, and pleasant. It's weird," Kiwi said.

Noora giggled again. She'd missed their banter.

Her mother started picking up on Noora's reactions.

"Dax," Noora's father said. "Noora says you're the ship's engineer? Are you a technician?"

Noora bit her lip, knowing her father's stoic English could come off as rude.

But Dax wasn't offended. "Both, actually. I'm an engineer by trade, but when you're on a ship, you're more technician than anything."

Noora leaned into Dax. "My dad is also an engineer," she said.

"Oh, no kidding," Dax said. "What do you do?"

"I'm a manager now, so I don't do design anymore, but I work for a company that does ship design out of Turku. It's west of here."

"Nice," Dax said. "I did interplanetary engine design for years. And then, um, and then life happened, and I decided to go interplanetary myself."

Kiwi quietly sipped her beer, knowing Dax was referring to his deceased wife, knowing she was the only one at the table who knew that.

"Hänellä on mukavat kädet [he does have nice arms]," Noora's sister said to her, quietly.

Noora sniped her with a look. Luckily, her parents hadn't heard Niina's comment.

"What was that?" Dax asked.

"Oh," Noora stuttered. "Sorry, she was just saying it's cool you're an engineer."

"Sorry," Niina said awkwardly in English. "I'm not used to speaking English."

"No apologies," Dax said, raising his mead. "Cheers."

Niina, charmed, raised her glass. "Cheer!"

"This pork and this salmon are so goddamn good, and this *bread!*" Kiwi said. "Dax, how come you don't cook like this?"

"Because those of us from East Texas aren't as cultured as the rest of the world," Dax said without missing a beat.

Noora giggled again, leaning into Dax.

Niina tried to give Noora a look to let her know she was giving too much away.

But Noora was a lightweight, and the mead was getting to her.

Kiwi's phone buzzed. "Oo! It's Eddie!" she squealed, typing into her phone.

Noora's jaw dropped. "Not, oh my god, not Raikkonen!"

Noora's mother, father, and sister all looked stunned.

"Wait, I'm sorry," Noora's father said. "*Edvard* Raikkonen?"

Noora looked at him and nodded.

"Hey," Kiwi said. "He's been bugging me to hang out with him since I told him I'd be in Finland. Do you guys mind if he stops by?"

Dax scoffed. "The hell's wrong with you? We're guests here, you can't just invite someone else over."

"Are, are you serious?" Noora's father asked Kiwi. "Edvard Raikkonen?"

"Yeah!" Kiwi confirmed. "I mean, if it's okay, I don't want to be rude."

Noora's family got over their initial shock. "Well, *yes!*" her mother said.

"Of course!" her father said.

"Oh my god is he really coming?" her sister said.

"I mean, if that's cool," Kiwi said, typing away at her phone.

"Yes, of course!" Noora's father exclaimed.

Dax, confused, looked at Noora. "What's the big deal?"

"You don't understand," she said. "Finland has, like, no celebrities, and Raikkonen is our current celebrity."

Dax whispered. "You're not gonna tell anyone we tried to blow out his tires, are you?"

Noora remembered how she'd already told her sister about that. "No?" she said.

"Eddie!" Kiwi greeted outside Noora's house. "Thank you for coming!"

"Of course," Edvard Raikkonen said, giving Kiwi a quick hug.

"Come in, come in!" Kiwi squealed.

Edvard followed her inside.

Noora's family were all stunned. The biggest celebrity in Finland was now in their house.

"Mr. Raikkonen," her father said in Finnish. "It's so wonderful to meet you."

"Mr. Raikkonen, can I get you anything?" her mother asked.

"Holy shit it's fucking Raikkonen," her sister said under her breath.

Edvard introduced himself to Noora. "Hi, nice to meet you," he said in Finnish.

"No, it's just, wonderful to meet *you*," she said.

Edvard then introduced himself to Dax. He could tell Dax was American from his demeanor, and said in English, "Hello. Nice to meet you."

"Sup, I'm Dax," Dax said.

"Dax, thank you," Raikkonen said.

They all sat at the dining table, trading stories in English and Finnish, Noora doing her best to translate when she could.

Dax was enjoying himself, but the cross-talk was starting to get to him.

"Here, lemme get these outta the way," he said, gathering up some of the dishes.

"Oh, no, please leave them, it's all right," Noora's mother said.

"It's cool, I got it," he said. But Noora's mother accompanied him to the kitchen.

"Just leave them in the sink," she said.

But Dax was hoping to clean them just so he could enjoy some time alone. "No, please," he said. "You made all this great food, least I can do is help clean up."

Dax was tall, assertive, and polite, and Noora's mother took him at his word.

"Well here, let me help," she said, getting the dish rack ready. "May I ask, why did your ship hire Noora?"

Dax didn't know what to disclose, so kept it vague. "You'll have to ask my captain. He needed a sharpshooter for an event on Mars, he decided she was a good fit for the crew, and made her an offer."

Noora's mother nodded. "And what do *you* think of Noora?" she asked, having noticed the way Noora had been looking and giggling at him.

"Me?" Dax asked, hearing her underlying question, cleaning a dish to buy himself some time for a proper answer. "I mean, she gets along with Kiwi, which is the most important part of fitting in with the ship. Yeah, Noora's great."

Noora's mother nodded, then said, "It's just, I wonder why Noora's *really* going back out into space."

Dax understood the insinuation. He put down the dishes and looked at Noora's mother. "Look," he said, holding up his left hand. "I know I don't wear the ring, but I was married 17 years ago. I don't know what you think about Americans, but I'm *boringly* monogamous. Noora's a great addition to the crew. Our captain offered her a position, and she accepted."

Noora's mother nodded, appreciating Dax's sincerity. "Oh, okay," she said. "But seriously, thank you, but please leave the dishes."

Dax respected her request, dried his hands, and returned to the dining room.

Everyone was fawning over the famous Finnish rally car racer, Edvard Raikkonen, except for Noora, who fawned over Dax once he entered the room. She invited him back to his chair.

"And then I said!" Kiwi shouted, giddy and partially drunk. "And then I said, 'does it look like I'm going anywhere?'"

Everyone who had been there for the joke laughed.

Dax sat down. Noora gently touched his shoulder.

Niina leaned into Noora. *"Kerro vain hänelle* [just tell him]," she said.

Noora shot her younger sister another glare.

Dax's phone rang. It was Gideon. He got up and went outside.

"Hey, captain, the hell you want?"

"Hey," Gideon said. *"Thought I'd call one of you, and turns out you're all in fucking Finland?"*

"I love it when you track our phones," Dax said.

"Captain's prerogative."

"So what do you want?" Dax asked.

"I want you all to get your arses to Macedonia as soon as you can."

"The hell's a Scotsman doing in Macedonia?" Dax asked.

"The hell's an East Texan doing in Finland?"

"Fair enough," Dax conceded.

"When do you think you can get the girls here?"

"It's more a question of when I can detach Kiwi from her Finnish boy toy," Dax said. "Dunno, gimme, like, a day or two?"

"That's fine. Just keep me posted on when you get here."

"Roger roger," Dax said, before hanging up.

Noora was behind him. "Hey," she said. "Everything all right?"

"Yeah," Dax said. "That was Gideon. Wants us to join him when we can."

"Oh, okay," Noora said, trying to hide her excitement. "Did he say when?"

"Soon. We just gotta separate Kiwi from Eddie."

Noora let loose a playful scoff. "Well, I mean, good luck with that."

Dax laughed.

Noora laughed, too. "Thanks for coming," she said.

"Thanks for having us," Dax said.

Noora rubbed his arm, and they entered the house.

But Noora's mother took her aside. "Noora, can we talk for a moment?" she asked in Finnish.

"Oh, um, sure."

Once Dax had left the vicinity, her mother said. "I just wanted you to know that we love you, and we trust you, and I know your father and I aren't crazy about you going back out into space, but just keep in touch with us, okay?"

Noora felt a great relief off her perfectly cut shoulders. "Thank you, mom," she said.

"You know," her mother said. "I thought you and Dax were a thing, but I was talking with him in the kitchen, and I hadn't realized he's married."

Noora's jaw dropped to the ground. *"What!"*

16. A Nightclub in Macedonia

Kiwi gets in trouble with the Macedonian mafia, Dax claims to have a small penis, Noora doesn't know what to do, and Gideon pays 18-grand.

"Hello," a large Macedonian greeted Dax, flanked by another stocky Macedonian.

"Hello," Dax said, eating his eggs in the hotel lobby.

"We're here to kill your friend," the large Macedonian declared.

Dax played it cool. Without putting down his fork, he said, "Okay, which one?"

"She is short one," the Macedonian said. "Have long, black hair."

Dax nodded, knowing they were referring to Kiwi. He kept calm. "I mean, I don't blame you. Sometimes I wanna kill her myself."

The large Macedonian, just as tall as Dax and built of brick, sat down. "Look," he said. "We have seen video of last night. *You* did nothing wrong, but your friend threw my niece over table, so you will tell us where your friend is now, or we will kill you, too."

Dax nodded, keeping his poker face. He could tell they were not bluffing. "Well I can text her."

"What room she in?"

"Dude," Dax said. "One, I don't know, and two, I doubt she's even in this hotel. She's probably shacked up with whatever asshole she hooked up with last night." Dax was lying. He knew Kiwi and Noora were rooming together in this hotel, but he didn't remember the room number, and he wouldn't be surprised if Kiwi had gone out again after the club incident last night. He came off as genuine.

The large Macedonian nodded, sizing Dax up. "I believe you," he said. "You honorable man. My niece, she try to seduce you last night. We saw on video. But you turn her down. Then your friend throw her over table. Please, text your friend."

Dax, making sure his movements were slow and casual, pulled out his phone, and texted both Kiwi and Noora.

Stay in your fucking room. Do not come out. Two guys are here to kill Kiwi. I'm not joking.

"You know what?" Dax said. "I can give my captain a call, too. He might know where she is."

"Yes. Please do this."

Gideon's phone rang, startling him awake. The woman next to him made some half-conscious noises, but was soon back asleep.

He saw it was Dax. "You have a good reason for waking me up?" he answered.

"I sure do, captain. I'm in the lobby with a couple of gentlemen. They were hoping to kill Kiwi."

Gideon scowled, thinking Dax was pranking him, but could tell from his tone that he was serious. "Oh shit, you're serious."

"You better believe it."

"What the fuck happened last night? I told you to keep an eye on Kiwi and Noora!"

"And I've told you before there's no chaperoning her when she goes clubbing."

"Christ, well where is she now?"

"No idea, that's what we're trying to find out."

"I take it from your tone that those two gentlemen are with you and are listening to you right now?"

"And you would be right, and I really don't want to keep them waiting."

"Well keep them there for now. I'm on my way down."

He hung up and got out of bed. The woman in his bed squirmed slowly. "Where you go?" she asked, half asleep.

"Just down to the lobby," Gideon said, getting dressed. "You go back to bed, I'll be back later." He pecked her on the cheek and made his way to the lobby.

Dax hung up. "My captain doesn't know where she is, either, but he is on his way down. Says he'd like to discuss it with you."

"*Just* your captain?" the large Macedonian asked.

Dax nodded, internally freaking out, but calmly taking another bite of his eggs. He reached for his coffee and said, "I'm sorry, here I am eating breakfast. Can I get you guys a pastry or some coffee?"

"Yes, coffee," the large one said. He turned around and shouted an order to one of the waitstaff, who shuddered, nodded quickly, and disappeared to the kitchen.

Dax had sized up the situation correctly from the start. Whoever this guy was, the locals knew not to fuck with him.

A waiter quickly came out with a copper carafe filled with Turkish coffee. "Here, let me," Dax said, taking the carafe and pouring some for the man sitting across from him. The more he could keep this pleasant civility going, the better.

"Thank you," the large man said.

Dax raised his own cup. "And may I say, I'm sorry for what Kiwi did to your niece last night."

"Kiwi? Who is this? Black-haired girl?"

Dax nodded.

"My niece, we saw on video she put hands on you. She say something to you. What she say to you?" the large Macedonian asked, sipping his coffee.

"She, um," Dax said, thinking about how to phrase what she said tactfully, but decided a direct quote would be better. "She said, 'Hey you, American, how big is that American dick?'"

"Heh heh," the large Macedonian chuckled, before erupting into an echoing guffaw. "My niece! She party too much, drink too much! Act like slut! My brother, he spoil her, never teach her how to behave! But it's good you not touch her, or we must kill you, too!" He kept laughing.

"And we wouldn't want that, would we?" Dax said, pretending to laugh along.

Gideon entered the lobby and carefully approached Dax's table. The stocky Macedonian eyed him. Dax stood up, hoping to keep things calm. "Ah, here's my captain, Gideon. Gideon, I'd introduce you, but I didn't get the gentleman's name."

"Bogdan," the large Macedonian said, shaking Gideon's hand.

"Bogdan, I'm Gideon," he said. "I'm sorry for any trouble my crewman caused, can you tell me what happened?"

They all sat down. Bogdan pulled out his phone. "I *show* you what happened." He called up a video and played it.

"This is so cool! This might be my favorite club yet!" Kiwi shouted over the music. "Are you having fun?"

"Yeah!" Noora said, glancing at Dax, who sat at the bar. "Dax doesn't seem to be having fun, though!"

"Don't worry, he hates fun! Here, lemme get us another round!"

Noora went over to Dax, putting a hand on his shoulder. "Thanks for coming. I hope you're not bored."

"Gideon didn't gimme a choice," Dax said.

A young woman in a cocktail dress, surrounded by friends, laughed obnoxiously a few seats down the bar.

Noora sneered. Whoever she was, she'd been eyeing Dax.

"Well thank you anyway," Noora said.

"Don't worry about it. I mean he's right. He told us to watch ourselves while we're here, and with Kiwi, you never know—"

The obnoxious young woman had stumbled over and wedged herself between Noora and Dax.

"Hey!" Noora exclaimed.

The young woman rubbed a hand on Dax's arm and another up his thigh.

"Oooo, you American!" she slurred, slobbering drunk. "How big is that American dick?"

"Small," Dax said. "Go away."

"Pfff!" Noora chortled, unable to hide her laugh.

"Ohhh, what wrong!" the young woman shouted. "You no like woman?"

Kiwi returned with drinks, not liking what she was seeing.

"What, you *gay*? You can't get woman with your *small* dick? Fuck you!"

"The fuck did you say to him!" Kiwi shouted, splashing both drinks on the young woman, grabbing her, and throwing her over a bar-side table. *"Fucking whore!"*

Noora was too shocked to know what to do.

Dax grabbed Kiwi. "The *fuck* are you doing!"

"Drunk slut can't be saying that shit to you!"

"Jesus *Christ!* We're in Macedonia, we don't know who's who, and Gideon told us to watch it while we're out!"

The young woman's troupe went to her, trying to help her up. They eyed Kiwi and Dax, but knew not to try anything. The young woman, makeup ruined, drenched and banged up, slowly got up and cried, "Fucking *bitch!* Fucking bitch, my uncle fucking *kill* you! He *kill* you, bitch!"

One of the bouncers had finally made it to Kiwi. "You must leave. Now."

"On our way out," Dax said, grabbing Kiwi by the wrist.

"Hey!" Kiwi objected as Dax dragged her to the exit, Noora tagging along.

"We're going back to the hotel, and you're fucking grounded," Dax said.

The video ended, and Bogdan put his phone away. "So you see, black-haired girl, Kiwi, she throw my niece."

Gideon looked at Dax. "What did that woman say to you? What set Kiwi off?"

"She came up to me, slid a hand up my thigh to my crotch, asked me how big my dick was, I told her to go away, she didn't like that, so she told me I was gay and that I can't get a woman because of my small dick. Kiwi didn't like that, so, you know."

"My niece," Bogdan said. "She say that to you?"

Dax nodded.

Bogdan knew Dax was telling the truth. "She lie. Tell me black-haired girl throw her for no reason. This not surprise. Niece lie all the time."

"Look," Gideon said, "I want to make things right for you and your niece. My crewmember, Kiwi, was wrong."

"Dah," Bogdan scoffed, waving a hand. "Niece deserve it. About time someone smack her. Tell you what, friend, you are very respectful, I like this. For 20,000, I can let Kiwi go."

"20?" Gideon said. "A bit steep. How does 15 sound?"

Bogdan gave it some thought. "18, but only because I like this gentleman here," he said pointing at Dax. "And make sure Kiwi goes to no more club while here. Best she not go out at all."

"No argument from me," Gideon said. He queued up his phone and tapped it to Bogdan's, transferring the 18,000.

Bogdan got up, in a cheerful mood. "I'm sorry I interrupt breakfast," he said to Dax.

"Not an interruption," Dax said, raising his coffee, still playing cool. "Thanks for joining me."

Bogdan produced a business card and gave it to Dax. "My restaurant. You stop by. We make you lunch, dinner, whatever you want. Our treat."

"Well thank you," Dax said, accepting the card.

Bogdan and his stocky companion left.

Dax let out a huge sigh. "Jesus *fucking* Christ. Were they really gonna kill her?"

"Eh, you never know with the Macedonian mafia," Gideon said. "Usually they say they're gonna kill you, but they're really just shaking you down for money."

Dax received a text. Noora had finally gotten back to him. *Oh my fucking god are you serious?! Kiwi & I are in our room. She just woke up. What do we do?!!*

Dax texted back: *Stay calm. Don't leave the room. I'll be up in a bit.*

"Well, Kiwi and Noora are still in their room," he said.

"Good, make sure Kiwi, at least, stays there for now. I'm going back up to my room for a bit, then I gotta head out. Lunch meeting with my contact for our next gig."

"Why the hell did we have to come here, anyway?"

"Because my contact here is more traditional. He prefers face-to-face, and doesn't like communicating over the airwaves. And I got the impression he wants us to fly as soon as we're done talking over the details, so that's why I wanted the rest of you here."

"Well," Dax said, standing up. "Guess I'll be on guard duty."

"Make sure to tell Kiwi she owes me 18-grand."

"Where are they?" Kiwi asked as Noora let Dax into the room. "I'll kill 'em both."

"They're gone, you owe Gideon 18-grand, and you owe me bypass surgery for the fucking heart attack I just had downstairs." He sat down and made himself comfortable.

"What the heck happened!" Noora asked.

"That sultry Slavic woman you threw into a table last night turns out to be the niece of a local Macedonian mafioso. Gideon paid 18-grand for them not to kill you."

"Dax, you can't be letting girls say that shit to you," Kiwi said.

"It's the only way women know how to insult guys!" Dax shot back. "The only insulting thing about it is it's such a *boring* insult."

"So, um, are they gone now?" Noora asked.

"Yes. Noora, you're free to come and go as you please. Kiwi, you really *are* grounded now."

"Bull shit!" Kiwi exclaimed.

"Hey, when your local organized criminal suggests that you do something, it's not a suggestion. He said it's best if you stay here while we're in town, and that's *exactly* what you're gonna do."

Kiwi rolled her eyes and sighed. "Fine. I hope you enjoy running around getting me food and liquor."

"If that's what it takes, yes," Dax confirmed, pulling out his phone to pass the time. "Lemme know when you're hungry for lunch. I already got a local restaurant in mind."

Gideon made it to the pre-arranged meeting place, a restaurant not far from the hotel, only to be shocked at the voice that greeted him.

"Gideon!" Bogdan shouted. "You come to my place! What you need?"

"Oh, hey, Bogdan," Gideon said, shaking his hand. "Yeah, no, I actually came here to meet a, uh, to meet someone." He looked around for his contact, finding him, and waving.

Bogdan saw who he waved to. "Dmitry! You know Dmitry? Why you not tell me this? Whole thing with niece, forgotten!" Bogdan walked Gideon over to Dmitry's table. The two of them laughed, exchanging a few words in Macedonian. Bogdan slapped Gideon on the back and took off.

Gideon sat down, shaking Dmitry's hand. "How ya been?" he asked.

"Good," Dmitry said, his accent a mix of mild-Macedonian and British. "Good to see you again." He poured Gideon a measure of Turkish coffee. "How do you know Bogdan? He talks about you like you're best friends."

"Well I just paid him 18 grand to not kill one of my crew members, so I'd say we're on good terms."

"Ha! What did your crew member do?"

"Threw his niece into a table."

"Oh yeah," Dmitry nodded. "*That* bitch. Trust me, she deserved it."

Gideon managed a laugh. "Anyway, tell me what you got lined up for me."

Dax had looked up Bogdan's restaurant on his phone, found it was only half a mile from the hotel, and walked there to pick up lunch.

"Oh! What is this! You come, too!" Bogdan greeted him.

Dax was confused, but greeted him all the same. "I mean, just thought I'd come pick up some lunch."

"Your captain, Gideon, he here, too."

Dax scowled in confusion. "Oh, okay."

"What you need?" Bogdan asked.

"For lunch? I mean, I don't know, I need enough for three people. Take out. Whatever you recommend."

Bogdan turned around and barked some orders to his kitchen staff, all of whom nodded and quickly got back to work.

Dax looked around for his captain, found him, saw he was in deep conversation with someone, and decided not to bug him.

But Bogdan had other ideas. "Here, come!" he said. "Your captain this way!"

Dax followed, worried about interrupting Gideon unannounced. He never was involved in the deals his captain set up, and preferred to keep it that way.

"Look who come by!" Bogdan announced.

"Hey captain," Dax said. "Sir," he said to the other gentleman. "Sorry, just took up Bogdan on his food offer, didn't realize you'd be here."

"No, actually, this is perfect, have a seat," Gideon said.

Dax sat down.

"I was just talking with Dmitry here. Dmitry, this is my ship's engineer."

Dax and Dmitry introduced each other and shook hands.

"Dax, can you tell me," Gideon said. "What would it take to make the *Isle of Skye* go interstellar?"

Dax was stunned at the question. He thought for a second, then just started talking. "I mean, *whew*, you'd need a second reactor just for the vector drive. And I don't know if you know this, but a second reactor by itself is expensive, and an interstellar vector drive costs a fortune. And we'd need a new modulated shielding system, can't fly interstellar without one. Then there's installation," Dax said, shrugging. "Probably a week or two to install everything, and that's assuming you can get all of it quickly."

Gideon nodded. "Think you can get me a cost estimate today?"

Dax exhaled. "Um, yeah. And seriously, it'd just be an estimate."

"That's all I need," Gideon said.

Bogdan returned. "You, sir, we have your lunch ready."

"Oh, um, thank you," Dax said standing up. "Are you guys good, or?"

Gideon nodded.

"Pleasure to meet you, Dax," Dmitry said.

"So, like, can I ask you?" Noora said to Kiwi, finally working up the courage to ask. "Did you, um, like, did you know that Dax was married?"

Kiwi looked up from her phone. "I mean, look, I only found out, like a week ago, when I went to pick him up in Texas."

Noora smacked a fist into her thigh. "Goddammit."

"What do you mean?" Kiwi asked, confused.

"Well it would've been nice to know that, Kiwi!"

"Noora, what the fuck. He *was* married."

Noora heard Kiwi's emphasis. "Wait. Wait, *was?*"

"Yeah, *was.*"

"So, is he, like, divorced or something?"

Kiwi put her phone down. Her tone got serious. "No, he's um, I'm sorry. Like I said, he *was* married. His, um, his wife died years ago."

Noora took a sharp inhale, her hands coming to her mouth. "Oh my god."

"Yeah, like, look, like I mentioned, I just found out about this myself. It's kinda sad. He was married for, like, 14 years, and his wife fucking dies, and his boss tried to fire him, but he quit anyway, found a job with Gideon to go traveling around in space because he hates people and wants to be alone and that's why he's always, like, dark and brooding and doesn't give a fuck about anything anymore."

Noora's hands were still on her mouth. "Oh my god," she said.

There was a knock at the door. Kiwi went to answer it.

Dax entered, carrying a hefty bag of lunch.

"All right," he said. "Don't know what we have, but we got a lot."

"Oooo! Lunch!" Kiwi squealed.

"Yeah, um, thank you, Dax," Noora said awkwardly.

"Eat up," Dax said. "Because we're going interstellar."

"What?" Kiwi shouted.

"What?" Noora said.

"You heard me."

17. Unexpected Guest

Gideon has cargo trouble, Dax is covered in grease, Kiwi cries, Noora cries, Philly Cheesesteak flicks his tail, and the Isle gets a refit.

Philly Cheesesteak was not enjoying the screeching of the dropship docking with the *Isle*. He had been grumpy the whole trip.

"Knock it off," Kiwi chided him. "I asked if you wanted to stay on the farm, and you said you wanted to come with me. I told you we're going interstellar and I don't know where to, and you said *'myah, Kiwi, I wanna come, too, myah.'*"

"*Myah,*" Philly Cheesesteak protested.

"Besides, I thought the *Isle* was still in Earth orbit. They didn't tell me they'd be out here dry-docked on the fucking moon."

Kiwi finished the docking procedure, normalized the pressure, and opened the hatch to the *Isle*.

Only to be greeted by metallic clanging echoing through the ship's hull.

Philly Cheesesteak ran straight to an air vent to hide.

Kiwi pulled out her phone and patched into the *Isle's* intercom. "Dax? Gideon? Anyone here? The hell's going on with all the noise."

"Oh hey," Dax answered in a bad mood. *"You took your sweet-ass time getting here!"*

"Oh for Christ's sake, get the sand out of your vagina, Dax! Where are you, engineering?

"I've been holed up in engineering for a fucking week."

"No wonder you're in such a good mood. Gimme a minute, I'll be right there."

"Hi, Kiwi!" Noora shouted over the noise.

"Hey, girl! You with Dax? I'll see ya in a second!"

Kiwi made her way to engineering. Whatever the cacophony was, it was coming from there.

She arrived, and promptly blurted out, "Holy shit!"

A dozen technicians she didn't recognize were scurrying around, installing massive new machinery and technology she also didn't recognize. She looked around for Dax, and found him sticking out from underneath a new plasma junction.

"No no no," Dax said to a technician squeezed under the junction with him. "Route that through *here*."

Kiwi gently kicked his leg. "Hey, asshole!" she shouted over the noise. "Do I get a hug or what?"

Dax pushed himself out, got up, and threw a grease-covered arm around Kiwi, giving her a hug. "There, ya happy?"

"Happier than you, Mr. Grumpy!"

"I've never been happy, and you know that."

"Kiwi!" Noora shouted, coming up from behind.

"Hey, girl!" Kiwi shouted back, trying to give her a hug.

"Oh, no, I'm so dirty," Noora said, dirt and grease on her face.

"It's okay, Dax already greased me up!" she said, giving Noora a friendly hug. She let go and said, "Let's go into the corridor, it's too fucking loud in here!"

The trio left engineering and sealed the door behind them. "So, uh, holy shit. What the hell are you guys doing to engineering?" Kiwi asked.

"Installing the vector drive that lets us fly interstellar, installing a new shield modulating system so we don't fly apart, and installing a second reactor to power it all," Dax answered.

"There's hardly any space left in there," Kiwi said. "And how's Gideon paying for it? All that shit costs more than the *Isle* is worth."

Dax shrugged.

"How was your trip?" Noora asked. "Is Philly Cheesesteak with you?"

"Yeah, but he didn't like the noise, so he's hiding in the air vents. He'll come out later," Kiwi said. "So, after I get all my shit off the drop ship, I assume you want some help?"

"I don't know," Dax said. "Noora's been helping out a bunch, and she actually listens to me and doesn't talk back."

Noora blushed underneath the dirt and grease on her face. "Oh, I mean, I've been learning a lot, actually, and I've just been like, fetching stuff. Speaking of, I'm running to cargo, do you need anything, Dax?"

Dax's tone suddenly became gentle. "Oh, no, I'm good, but thank you."

Noora nodded, quickly touched his arm, and took off.

After she was gone, Dax said, "You told her, didn't you?"

"What, that you were married?" Kiwi asked. "Well, actually her mom told her, and she thought you were, like, still married. And I told her, you know, that you're a widower."

Dax nodded. "Yeah, I figured. She's been extra sweet to me since Macedonia."

Kiwi raised an eyebrow. "Are you guys, finally…?"

"No," Dax said. "And stop trying to play matchmaker. Now go get your shit off the drop ship and get your ass back here. I wanna try to finish this up before Gideon gets back, and I wanna show you how everything works."

"Where *is* Gideon, anyway?" Kiwi asked.

"He's off seeing whatever cargo it is we're gonna be transporting."

"What *are* we transporting?"

"Don't know."

"And where are we going?"

"Don't know."

Gideon rubbed his forehead and let loose a huge sigh. He was in a lunar warehouse, staring at the sea of cargo, wondering how he was going to fit it all on the *Isle*.

"And you said *all* of it?" he asked.

"All of it," Dmitry confirmed in his British-Macedonian accent.

"I, uh, okay," Gideon stuttered, knowing he couldn't say no.

"What's wrong?"

"No, it's just, there's no way I can fit this all in my cargo bay. I'll need to fill the corridors, the rec room, the mess hall, every room is gonna have to be stacked with crates."

"But you *can* fit it all?" Dmitry asked.

Gideon exhaled again. It was gonna be a tight fit, and they couldn't even start loading until Dax was done refitting the ship. "We'll make sure we can."

Dmitry shook Gideon's hand. "When do you think you can load up and take off?"

Gideon pulled out his phone. "Lemme ask my engineer," he said, giving Dax a call.

"Yeah! What's up!" Dax shouted through a symphony of noise.

"Hey, I'm not rushing you, but how much longer do you think the refit is gonna take?"

"Well we're almost done for today, and we actually should be finished by tomorrow! New reactor is in, the vector drive is in, we're just making sure the ship won't blow itself apart when everything is running!"

"Thanks, mate. Keep it up," Gideon said, and hung up. He looked to Dmitry. "Looks like we'll finish up tomorrow. Can start loading the day after."

"Wonderful," Dmitry said. "Where's the *Isle* parked, again?"

"We're dry-docked in Alpine Valley for the refit, but it's a quick hop over here once we're done."

"Nice. Be in touch tomorrow," Dmitry said.

They parted ways.

Gideon left the warehouse and was about to make his way to an auto-taxi to get back to the *Isle*, when a familiar voice called to him. "Hey."

Gideon was startled at who he was looking at. "Hello, Jason."

Jason, who had chased Gideon's crew across the solar system, who had kidnapped Kiwi, captured himself and Dax, and who's ship Kiwi and Noora had shot up, stood before him, leaning against the wall, a large duffle bag hanging off his shoulder.

"How, uh, how ya been?" Jason asked.

Gideon glanced around the corridor, wondering if he was being flanked.

"It's just me," Jason said.

"I've, uh, I've been fine," Gideon said, not sure what to make of the situation. "Yourself?"

Jason shrugged. "I've been better."

"What's, uh, what's in the bag?" Gideon asked.

"Everything I own."

Gideon was starting to notice Jason's demeanor. He seemed defeated. "Did you, erm, did you end up losing your ship?"

Jason shook his head. "Wasn't my ship. Was my employer's."

Gideon nodded. "I see. I take it your employer wasn't happy that an engine got blown off?"

Jason nodded. "Yeah, you know, they um, they were less than happy with me."

"I take it it's no accident that you're also here on the moon, just waiting for me in this corridor?"

Jason nodded again.

"So what brings you here?"

Jason shrugged. "Looking for work."

Gideon scoffed, knowing Jason was asking him for a job. "Well good luck. The Lunar Port is always looking for forklift drivers." He started to leave.

"I'm blacklisted," Jason said.

Gideon stopped. He knew what that meant for the line of work he and Jason were in. "I see."

"Employer shitcanned me after, uh, well after what happened on Mars. Said they were gonna make sure I never worked again," Jason said.

Gideon could tell he was telling the truth. But rather than feel sympathy, he wondered if he could put Jason to work. "Well look," he said. "The rest of the crew isn't exactly happy with you, plus I don't know what you can do to contribute. So I tell you what, I'm about to head back to the *Isle*. We'll have a sit-down with everyone, and if we decide you can tag along, you won't get much, if any, of a paycheck, because I'm going into way too much debt with the refit we're doing."

"Yeah, I noticed," Jason said, pushing off from the wall and following Gideon. "Installing a vector drive, huh?"

Gideon frowned. "How'd you know that?"

"I'm good at finding out things," Jason said.

"You know, I never got a last name for you," Gideon said.

"Dufresne."

"What in the goddamn tits is fuckboy doing here!" Kiwi shouted as Gideon and Jason entered the mess hall.

Dax, Noora, and Kiwi sat at a table. Philly Cheesesteak sat on the floor, and hissed when he saw Jason.

Dax was cautious.

Noora didn't know what was going on.

"Everyone calm down," Gideon said. He and Jason came to the table and sat down.

"Gideon," Dax said. "Whatever you're about to say, the answer is no."

"Did you lose your memory after he gave you a black eye, Gideon?" Kiwi said, voice still raised. She looked at Jason. "I should've shot up the rest of your ship."

Noora stayed quiet, starting to piece together who this person was.

"So yes, you all may recognize Jason, here," Gideon said. "He's been fired from his primary job of chasing us around the solar system, and would now like to come work with us."

Dax rolled his eyes. "Not to publicly agree with Kiwi, but she has a fucking point. We can't trust this guy. Why the hell did you even let him on the ship?"

"Call it a mercenary's intuition," Gideon said.

Jason was unfazed. He opened his duffle bag, routed around for a bit, pulled out a jet-injector, and placed it on the table.

Everyone was confused, but Kiwi recognized it. "Lemme guess. That *truthinol* shit."

Jason nodded. "Pump me full of it. Ask me anything. You'll see I'm telling the truth."

Dax scoffed. "You expect us to believe that?"

Kiwi snatched the jet-injector. "Only one way to find out," she said, adjusting the dosage for a 93-pound female.

"Kiwi are you fucking insane!" Noora shouted.

"Don't worry, I'll leave enough for fuckboy," Kiwi said. "Just in case this is poison, make sure he dies a slow death."

"Wait, wait, Kiwi—" Dax and Gideon both tried to say, before Kiwi held the injector to her neck and pulled the trigger.

"God fucking dammet," Dax said, smacking his forehead with his hand.

"She'll be fine," Jason said.

Kiwi put the injector back on the table. After a few seconds, she lost her balance even though she was still sitting down. Noora moved to grab her, but Kiwi caught herself. "Whoah," she said, before she started to giggle. She looked around at everyone, a giddy mess. "Well gang! Ask me anything!"

"Why do you drink so much?" Dax asked.

"Daaaaax," Kiwi said playfully. "You know I drink because alcohol lights up my brain and because I take after my self-destructive mom. Next question!"

"You actually sound normal," Dax said.

"I don't feel normal," she said, swaying. "Ask me something else."

"When's the first time you had sex," Dax asked.

"Dax! Oh my god, that's so rude!" Noora exclaimed.

"I was 16," Kiwi said. "I fucked the farmhand my grandparents had hired. Right out in the barn, too. I think he was 18 or 19? Tall, lanky guy. They always have huge dicks. Anyway, I was 16 and horny, and my grandparents went out to the store, and I cornered him in the barn and—"

"Okay okay, we got it," Dax said.

"And speaking of *seeeeeeex*," Kiwi said, lowering her voice and pretending to whisper. "Dax, Noora wants to ride that hog of yours until she squeals."

Noora's face went into shock. Then she turned beet-red and tried to hide behind her left hand.

"No no, Noora, it's okay," Kiwi said. "I've almost talked Dax into doing you. Just give me some more time."

"Fuck you, Kiwi!" Noora shouted, before getting up and storming out of the mess hall.

"Wait, what?" Kiwi said, confused. "But it's not my fault! It's the drug!" she shouted, before snapping into a ball of rage. She slammed her hands on the table and screamed. *"IT'S NOT! MY! FAULT!"* She got up and ran after Noora, and started sobbing uncontrollably. "Noora! Noora, I'm so, I'm so sorry! Please!"

Gideon looked at Jason. "You sure you want a job?"

Jason raised his eyebrows. "Now you got me wondering."

Dax pushed the jet-injector over to Jason. "Time to shoot up, fuckboy," he said.

"Now, I don't think there's a need for that," Gideon said.

"Gideon, if he doesn't shoot up or if I don't like his answers, I will physically throw him off this ship," Dax said.

"He's right," Jason said to Gideon. He took the injector and shot a dose into his neck. He put the injector down, and braced himself for the waves of dizziness. "God,

I hate this shit." He slumped onto the table, but slowly pushed himself up, showing a drowsy, drunken face.

"What exactly *is* that stuff?" Dax asked.

"Truthinol. Was developed by Stirling Pharma as a new anesthesia, but it doesn't so much knock people out as make them spill their darkest secrets. Shuts down executive function in the brain, too, but can also make people emotional, as you just saw. Basically alcohol on steroids. Since they couldn't sell it as an anesthesia, they sell it mostly to governments, and people like us. My last employer makes everyone take it before they hire you."

"Who was your last employer?" Gideon asked.

"Independent contractor through Ralston Corp," Jason said.

"What's that?" Dax asked.

"Mercenary contractor," Gideon answered. "They contract you to find us?"

Jason nodded. "They said Stirling Pharma was robbed out at their Uranus plant. Stirling goes through Ralston. Ralston contacts me a day after it happened. I was on Titan station, so they figured whoever robbed them would be headed there since it's the next closest thing to Uranus. I bribed one of the air traffic controllers to tip me off to any ship coming in from that direction. I also had Kiwi's description. Found her easily once she stepped onto the station."

"What happened after Titan?" Dax asked.

"Well, Ralston wasn't happy you guys got away. They have a reputation they like to keep. We tried to follow you to Mars, and we all know how that turned out."

"And what happened to your ship after Kiwi and Noora shot it up?" Dax asked.

Jason shook his head. "Not my ship. Ralston's. Anyway, engine number four was torn off. We limped to Mars Orbital and had to dry-dock for repairs. A guy for

Ralston told me I was done and that I wouldn't be working for any contractor ever again."

"How do we know Ralston isn't still after us?" Dax asked.

Jason shook his head again. "Maybe I don't work for them anymore, but I still have my contacts there. After you shot up the ship, they decided you were more trouble than you were worth. They closed the contract and refunded Stirling."

Gideon nodded. Dax exhaled in relief. "What kind of talent stack do you have?" Gideon asked.

"I'm great at logistics and tracking things, and research."

"Are you really okay with not getting a paycheck?" Gideon asked.

"Yes," Jason said, squeezing his eyes shut and shaking his head. The drug was getting to him. "I'm blacklisted, so I'll work for free until you can recommend me to someone who'll hire me."

Gideon looked at Dax. "You satisfied?"

"Maybe," Dax said. "When's the first time you had sex?" he asked Jason.

"19," Jason said. "My dad paid for me to get an escort."

Both Gideon and Dax lifted their eyebrows.

Jason rubbed his eyes. He looked uncomfortable. "Hey, you have a room I can sleep this off in? This stuff is just, man."

"Yeah, lemme take you to one," Dax said. He escorted Jason out, but was back in the mess hall in two minutes. "I put him in the room across from Kiwi."

"So, what do you think?" Gideon asked.

"I still don't like it, but hey, he seems to be telling the truth."

Gideon looked at Philly Cheesesteak. "And what do *you* think?"

Philly Phil flicked his tail, but slowly closed his eyes and looked away, echoing Dax's sentiment.

"Good," Gideon said. "That just leaves our current crew crisis to figure out. You wanna talk to Kiwi?"

"No," Dax said. "I'll go check on Noora. You check on Kiwi."

"It's me," Gideon announced before entering Kiwi's room.

Kiwi was balled up on her bed, sobbing.

"Hey, Rosevine. How are ya?"

"I always fuck things up!" she cried. "Noora fucking hates me! Dax fucking hates me! It's not my fault! That fucking drug! It makes you say shit you don't wanna say! I'm so *fucking* embarrassed!"

"Actually, you were right," Gideon said.

Kiwi rolled over and looked up. "What do you mean?"

"We didn't know what was in that jet-injector. Jason could've injected himself with saline and then acted the part. If we wanted to be sure, we needed to test it on one of us first."

Kiwi wiped at her swollen eyes. "See?" she said meekly, before slamming her face into a pillow. "I was *right*! I was fucking *right*! But the shit I said! Goddammet!"

"Calm down," Gideon said. He sat on the bed. "Get up, come here."

Kiwi sat up, wiped her face, and gave Gideon a hug.

"I'm sorry, Gideon."

"You don't owe me an apology at all," he said.

"Wait," Kiwi said. "Where's Dax?"

"He went to check on Noora."

Kiwi managed a chortle. "Pff, oh god, I'll bet that's gonna be awkward."

Dax had a feeling Noora wouldn't be checking her phone. He went to her room and chimed, but there was no answer. He checked the bridge, the cargo bay, the rec hall, and the armory.

He eventually found her tucked away in a corner of engineering, leaning against a bulkhead.

"Hey," he said.

"Oh, hey," she said back, wiping her eyes and sniffling. "I, uh, I'm sorry, I didn't hear you come in."

"Don't apologize."

"Look, um, Dax. I'm sorry, I'm so fucking embarrassed." She wiped her eyes again, then started crying in earnest. "I'm sorry, can I just be alone."

"I'm sorry, but no," Dax said.

Noora looked at him, and didn't know whether to giggle or to keep crying. so she did both.

Dax approached her, smiling at having made her laugh.

"It's just," Noora said. "I'm sorry Kiwi said that. Like, I'm mad at her, but it's kinda not her fault, but it kinda is, I don't know. Maybe space isn't for me." Her face wrinkled up and more tears came out.

Dax said nothing, and put his arms around her.

Noora stopped crying and took a sharp inhale. She slowly loosened up and slid her arms around him, too.

Dax held her for a while.

"Hey," he finally said. "You feel like hanging out tonight?"

Noora kept holding him. "Um," she said, sniffling a clot of snot out of her nose. "I mean, yeah. I'd love to."

18. Test Drive and Launch

Gideon has insomnia, Jason does some foreshadowing, Noora "sleepwalks," Dax scolds Philly Cheesesteak, and Kiwi plays some Wagner.

Gideon, Dax, and Jason stared at the ocean of cargo in the warehouse.

"You're joking," Dax said.

"No, I'm not," Gideon said.

"There's no way we're fitting all this," Dax said.

"Not all in the cargo bay," Gideon said, then turned to Jason. "You said you're good at logistics. How do we load and fit all this?"

Jason was already on his phone, calling up schematics for the *Isle*. He started strolling around the warehouse, looking at all the cargo. "Can you send me a manifest?" he asked Gideon.

Gideon pulled out his phone and sent Jason the manifest.

Jason punched away at his phone, still strolling around the warehouse, taking an occasional glance at all the sealed crates.

"Even if we *can* fit it all, you have any idea how heavy we're gonna be?" Dax asked.

Gideon queued up the manifest on his phone and showed it to Dax.

Dax did a double-take, making sure he counted the correct number of zeros on the total tonnage. "That, just—," he stuttered. "That's gonna increase our mass by 40%."

"I take it that's heavy?" Gideon asked.

"Even if we can fit it all in, I mean…" Dax said.

"Can we still take off?" Gideon asked.

"I mean, *yeah*, but—"

"And can we still fly?"

Dax loosed a massive exhale. "Yeah, but—"

Jason returned with a report. "Good news is yes, we can fit it all. The heavier, bigger stuff we'll secure in the cargo bay, but we'll also need to stack stuff in the armory, the rec room, the mess hall, the main corridors, and spare rooms if you gottem. You're also increasing the *Isle's* mass by about 40%. I don't know how that's gonna work for flying."

They both looked at Dax.

"Yeah, that's what I was getting at," Dax said. "Everything not in the cargo bay is gonna need to be strapped down. But I'm mostly worried about the gravity field. We're gonna be taxing the hell out of it with that much mass spread out around the ship. Yes, we can fly, but *Jesus,* acceleration, banking, any vector adjustment is gonna have to be done *slowly.*"

"I can give you a layout of where everything's going to be distributed," Jason offered.

"Yes, please."

"How long to load everything?" Gideon asked.

"Depends on how well the forklift operators listen to me," Jason said. "Maybe seven, eight hours to load everything."

"And how long to make all the modifications you need to the gravity and to strap everything down?" Gideon asked.

"Depends on how good a mood Kiwi's in," Dax said. "How was she when you saw her last night?"

"She'll be fine," Gideon said. "I told her to kiss and make up with Noora."

Dax nodded. "I told Noora the same."

Noora was in the rec hall doing a deadlift set, when Kiwi quietly and shamefully came in. Noora saw her, said, "Oh, hi," dropped the deadlift bar, and pulled out her earphones.

"Hey, I'm sorry. You're busy, I can talk later," Kiwi said.

"No, no, it's all right. How are you, um, how are you feeling after last night?"

"Yeah, I'm, uh, I'm fine, I just, um, I wanted to," Kiwi said, looking down, playing with her fingers, and starting to cry. "I'm just really sorry what I said last night, and like, I'm sorry I always fuck things up, I just feel really bad and, like, I hope we can still be friends, and—"

"Oh, no! It's okay!" Noora said, running up to Kiwi and giving her a hug.

Kiwi smiled through the tears, grateful for the hug.

"Actually, it's funny," Noora said. "I mean, yes, I was embarrassed, but like, I knew it was the drug and you couldn't help it. Anyway, I ran off to engineering, and Dax eventually found me, and he was really sweet."

Kiwi wiped away some tears and raised a skeptical eyebrow. "Dax was *sweet*?"

Noora blushed. "Yeah, he like, he held me for a while, and we were up super late last night just talking, and that was it. He was just so nice. I mean, like, we haven't even kissed or anything, it was just great to get to know him better, and he's already said we should hang out again tonight, and I don't know what I'm saying, maybe it's that, like, I hated it when you said that last night, but also if you hadn't, then I don't know, he and I wouldn't be getting to know each other like this. So I guess, maybe, thank you?"

Kiwi didn't know how to square what she was feeling with what Noora had just said. "Um, you're welcome?" she said.

Noora's smile burst into a laugh. Kiwi followed suit. They hugged each other again.

"Hey," Kiwi said. "I know this is a totally different topic, but I've been meaning to ask you. Can you, like, show me how you work out?"

"But, you already workout," Noora said. "And you look great."

"Yeah, but," Kiwi said. "But you're, like, you're cut, and I mean *cut*. It's just, I think it'd be fun to learn how you do what you do."

"Yeah," Noora said. "I'll tell you what, let's start—"

"Hey, Noora, Kiwi, you guys there?" It was Dax over the intercom.

"Oh, um, yeah, Dax!" Noora answered. "We're both here!"

"Awesome. We're gonna start loading the Isle in about 10 minutes. Jason's gonna be directing all the loading. We're gonna have forklifts in and out of here, main corridors included, so just keep an eye out as you need to move around the ship. And someone make sure Philly Cheesesteak is locked in one of your rooms. I don't want him getting run over by all the goddamn heavy machinery."

"Wait," Kiwi chimed in. "Why they running forklifts in the main corridors? How much cargo we taking on?"

"A lot," Dax said. *"I'll be back on board soon. When both of you are ready, meet me down in engineering. We need to figure out how to make the gravity generator not overload with all the extra mass we're taking on. Then*

once everything's loaded, we need to strap down anything not in the cargo bay."

"Kiwi exhaled. "Fuck me," she said under her breath. "This is gonna be a long day."

"Gideon," Kiwi said in the mess hall. "Really, I'm tired, and I kinda wanna just drink myself to sleep."

Dax, sitting next to her, arms crossed and eyes closed, grunted in agreement.

Noora, sitting next to Dax, head supported by her left arm, slowly blinked her eyes.

Jason, separated from the three of them, wiped his face and took a sharp inhale.

Philly Cheesesteak, grateful that the cacophony of the loading crew was gone, danced around everyone's legs, looking for attention.

"Well, we lift off tomorrow morning, so I'm briefing all of you now," Gideon said. He put his phone on the table and queued up his presentation to project onto the wall. "Tomorrow, we are lifting off from the moon, exiting lunar orbit, and setting a trajectory for Lacaille 9352."

Everyone perked up, interested in where they were going, except for Dax, whose arms remained crossed and eyes remained closed.

"It's a red dwarf," Gideon continued. "About 10.75 light years from here. There's a colony on the third planet, and it should take us about, how long do you think, Dax?"

Dax didn't respond.

"Dax!"

Dax snapped awake.

"How long to Lacaille 9352?"

"Oh yeah," Dax said, trying to rub his face awake. "Um, with this Gen II vector drive, we can do just over 1% of a light year per hour, so figure, what, about five weeks to get there."

"Five weeks!" Kiwi exclaimed.

"Holy shet," Noora said in her Finnish accent. "Five *weeks?*"

"Damn," Jason said, rubbing his eyes.

"Yeah," Dax continued, trying to wake himself up. "I mean, this technology is only 30 years old. I remember when I was a kid, the Gen I's worked, but were slower and more sketchy. A few of them flew out and were never heard from again. The Gen II's are faster and way more reliable."

"How *much* more reliable?" Kiwi asked.

"A lot more," Dax said.

Kiwi threw her arms up sarcastically. "Well *I'm* sold!"

"Where are we on the mass of the ship, the gravity field, all that?" Gideon asked.

Dax yawned. "Yeah, we um, we're good, just, like I said earlier, just do things like accelerating and turning as slow as you goddamn can, unless you wanna see the *Isle* shear itself apart."

"And what's that gonna mean for making it to Lacaille 9352?"

Dax yawned again. "Well, whatever relative speed we enter vector space, that's the same speed we *exit* vector space, so I need to figure out the ideal speed we need to enter Lacaille 9-something-or-whatever, and I need to make sure we do it at the right vector."

"And what will that take?" Gideon asked.

Dax gave a sharp exhale, not in the mood to calculate anything else. "I mean look, can I calculate this shit tomorrow? We can't even leave the solar system until we've spun up to whatever our ideal velocity is, and, I mean, just lemme do it tomorrow."

Gideon nodded, understanding how tired his crew was. "Yeah. Tomorrow." He looked to Jason. "In the meantime, scrounge up any info you have on Lacaille 9352. Get in touch with your contacts at Ralston if you have to."

Jason did a two-finger salute, then pulled out his phone.

"And one more thing," Gideon said. "Once we're in interstellar flight, there's no contacting anyone back home, because there's no such thing as faster-than-light radio. So message anyone you want to while we're still in the solar system."

Kiwi nudged Noora. "Hey, we gotta download all the episodes of *Tenjou Rayden* before we leave."

Noora was too shocked to hear what Kiwi had just said. "Oh my god. We'll be gone for that long? I have to send a message to my family."

Dax's arms were crossed and his eyes closed.

Jason was still doing research on his phone.

"So," Gideon said. "Now that there are no questions, all of you go get a good night's sleep."

"Meh-r-r-r-reow," Philly Cheesesteak said, stretching out.

Having showered and changed into their pjs, Dax and Noora were sitting on the floor in his room, leaning against the bed, talking and trying to stay awake.

"It's just," Noora said. "Don't you think it's weird that he's here? Like, the guy that captured you guys and whose ship we destroyed?"

"I mean, I didn't believe him at first," Dax admitted. "But everything about it makes sense, and besides him injecting himself with that truth serum, I don't know, there's something about him I trust."

"How can we, though?" Noora asked through a yawn. "Like, shouldn't you and Gideon and Kiwi all hate him?"

Dax shook his head, yawning himself. "That's the thing with guys. We can be rivals one day, and get along just fine the next." He got up onto his bed. He wanted to sleep, but didn't want to ask Noora to leave.

Noora got up on the bed as well, but stayed an arm's length away. "Is it all right if I stay?" she asked. "Just for a bit more?"

"Yeah, of course," Dax said, laying down. He felt a little awkward lying with her in bed, wondering if he needed to say anything else.

But Noora faded quickly. In seconds, her eyes were closed, her mouth was ajar, and her breathing was automatic and unconscious.

Dax smiled, feeling himself fade. He hadn't dated since he first started seeing Rochelle almost 20 years ago, and had no idea what to do. He could've kissed Noora by now. He could already be sleeping with her. Maybe he was holding back too much.

As he drifted to sleep, he thought how he would step things up tomorrow.

Gideon was in the mess hall, unable to sleep. The anxiety of interstellar flight was nagging him. It wasn't some glorious trek across the cosmos. It was long, claustrophobic, and isolating.

And it was risky. A number of speculators, eager to set up colonies with this new interstellar technology, had either failed or disappeared.

The few that did survive were often short on supplies, still struggling to set up their own economy. Most companies were reluctant to establish shipping routes; there was too much risk for too little return. The cost of insuring the ship and cargo of even one trade expedition was exorbitant.

But the occasional private businessman or mercenary could get around that. A few had made a fortune doing it.

Gideon poured himself another single malt, scrolled through the cargo manifest again, and scratched Philly Cheesesteak, who was laying down on the table.

"Hey, Gideon, you in the mess?" It was Jason over the intercom.

"Yeah. What's up?"

"Some stuff I found out about Lacaille 9352 that you'll want to know."

"That fast, huh? Yeah, join me."

Jason showed up a minute later. He sat down at the table, earning a sneer and a tail-flick from Philly Cheesesteak. He eyed the cat, and kept his distance. "Can't sleep either, huh?"

"Not a wink," Gideon said. "Whatcha got for me?"

"So, Lacaille 9352," Jason said, queuing up his phone. "A red dwarf, almost 11 light years away. Third planet's just inside the habitable zone. Slightly bigger than Earth, but less dense. Gravity's about 4% lower. Thicker atmosphere, though, about one-and-a-half times that of Earth, but it's mostly nitrogen and CO_2, more methane than you might expect, and argon."

Gideon nodded. This was all information he knew.

"It's also frozen solid," Jason said. "Lots of water, but it's all locked up in glaciers. And for some reason a colony decided to set up shop there almost 20 years ago. They tried seeding it with cyanobacteria to convert all that CO_2 to oxygen, but it never took, so they're stuck with the atmosphere they got. I mean you don't even need a pressure suit to walk around. Just a thick jacket and an oxygen supply."

Gideon nodded again. "Get to the part that I need to know."

"Yeah, sorry, just wanted to be thorough," Jason said, scrolling through his phone. "Colony's in the side of a mountain. Lots of iron and aluminum deposits, enough for them to keep building out and expanding. Sorry, not interesting, lemme skip ahead."

Gideon sipped his single malt and gave Philly Cheesesteak a few pets.

"Here's what caught my attention," Jason said. "I didn't think Ralston would care about some small, frozen colony, but get this, last year a ship from there came to Earth and tried to contract with Ralston. Said there was an uprising, or coup, or something going on, and they needed a team of soldiers."

"Damn," Gideon said. "They must've been desperate to have come all the way back here."

"Indeed," Jason said. "Anyway, they didn't have the funds for a contract like that with Ralston, so they bought a bunch of surplus rifles and munitions and headed back to Lacaille."

Gideon stroked his beard. "Anything else?" he asked.

"Yeah. That same ship was back in Earth orbit not two months ago."

Gideon frowned. "Hell of a lot of back-and-forth. What's the name of the ship?"

"The *Morena*," Jason said. "Named after some Slavic goddess of winter, or something.

"Slavic, huh?" Gideon said, seeing the connection. "Lemme guess, the crew spent most of their time in Macedonia."

Jason was stunned. "Yeah. How'd you know?"

"Because that's where I got our contract for Lacaille in the first place."

"What do you think it means?" Jason asked.

"Don't know," Gideon said. He started having a bad feeling about what the *Isle* was getting into, but kept it to himself. He yawned, then rubbed his face. "Listen, thank you. Good work." He drained the rest of his scotch and stood up.

"So, tomorrow's the day, huh?" Jason asked.

"Tomorrow's the day," Gideon confirmed. "Thanks again. Go get some sleep."

Dax woke up. Noora was drowning him with her mouth. Her eyes were shut, and she was aggressive with her tongue.

He went with it, putting his arms around her, and returning her enthusiasm. He hadn't touched anyone since Rochelle, and had forgotten what it felt like to have this connection and intimacy with someone.

He was about to take off Noora's shirt when, eyes still shut, she suddenly stopped, flashed a smile, and collapsed onto his shoulder, her breathing heavy and unconscious.

Dax was shocked for a second, then he started giggling, realizing Noora had been asleep the whole time. He imagined how embarrassed she'd be if she knew what she had done, and kept giggling at the thought. He tried to stifle his laughter so he didn't shake her awake.

He slid one of her legs off so she wasn't straddling him anymore. She stirred, but stayed asleep in his arm.

Dax held her, kissed her forehead, and eventually drifted back to sleep himself.

"All I'm saying is you need to watch *Tenjou Rayden* with me and Noora," Kiwi said in the mess hall. "What the hell else are you gonna do for the next five weeks? Where is Noora anyway? She's usually up before I am."

"She's probably still asleep in my bed," Dax said without missing a beat.

Kiwi took a sharp, delighted inhale, covering her mouth with her hands. She pattered her hands rapidly, giving a quiet applause.

Dax looked at her and said, "You know nothing."

"I," Kiwi stuttered, zipping her mouth. "I know nothing."

"Besides, you and I are gonna be busy enough while we're flying to Lacaille."

Kiwi frowned. "Really?"

"Oh yeah," Dax said, sipping his coffee. "We got so much energy pulsing through the *Isle* now that I'll be surprised if we don't fly her apart. You and I are gonna need to monitor everything carefully while we're in transit."

"Okay," Kiwi nodded. "But you're still watching *Tenjou Rayden* with us."

Dax rolled his eyes.

Jason strolled into the mess. "Oh, hey, good morning," he said.

"Oh look, it's fuckboy," Kiwi said.

"The one and only," Jason said, pouring himself some coffee. He went to sit down at a different table.

"Hey," Dax said. "Don't be a stranger. Come sit with us."

Jason nodded, lifted his coffee in gratitude, and sat with Dax and Kiwi. "Thank you," he said.

Philly Cheesesteak jumped up on the table. He eyed Jason and flicked his tail in spite.

"Oh you calm down," Dax said, picking up on Philly Phil's body language. "He's part of the crew now, whether you like it or not."

Philly Cheesesteak blinked his eyes and looked away.

Jason gave Dax a quick nod, which Dax returned.

Just as Noora entered the mess hall.

"*Noor-r-ra!*" Kiwi exclaimed in her imitation Finnish accent.

"Hey, everyone," Noora said, glancing at Dax, and then waving at everyone else. She poured herself some coffee and joined them at the table.

"How'd you sleep?" Dax asked, trying not to wink. He had woken up before her, and had left a message on her phone, telling her to sleep in as long as she needed, and that he'd be in the mess hall.

"Oh, um, yeah, just fine," Noora said.

"Hello, kids," Gideon said, entering the mess. He also poured himself some coffee, then joined his crew at the table. "So, today's the day."

Dax raised his coffee. "Today's the day."

"Today's the day!" Kiwi clapped.

Jason raised his coffee, as did Noora.

"Dax, how soon can we take off?" Gideon asked.

"As soon as I can finish my coffee," Dax said.

"Nice," Gideon said. "Jason, I want you on the bridge with me when we launch. And Noora, I need a sniper's eye when we test-navigate the vector drive, so I need you on the bridge, too."

"Oh, okay," Noora said.

"Before that," Dax said. "I need Noora in engineering for about five minutes. I've got our course all plotted out already, just wanna go over that and some limitations of the new vector drive."

"Oh, um, yeah, sure, if that's okay, Gideon?"

"Of course."

"And actually," Dax said, standing up, coffee in hand. "I'm gonna head there now. Noora, come with me. And Kiwi," he said, giving her a stern look. "No rush to engineering. Take your time finishing your coffee."

Kiwi winked. "You got it, boss."

"Hey, Dax," Noora said, as they entered the engineering section. "I'm sorry about last night, I didn't mean to fall asleep, you know, and—"

Dax grabbed Nocra and kissed her. She reciprocated.

When they separated, Noora was a happy, ruddy mess. She poked Dax's chest. "You're not gonna believe this. I had this dream last night where, like, you and I were making out like teenagers."

Dax laughed.

"What's so funny?" Noora asked, giddy.

"That wasn't a dream," Dax said.

Noora's eyes widened. "No! Oh my god, was I, like, sleepwalking? Or more, like, sleep-kissing?"

Dax nodded. "Yes."

Noora covered her eyes for a moment in shame, then looked up at Dax and asked, "Well, was I any good?"

"I didn't want you to stop."

Noora raised an eyebrow. "Maybe tonight I won't."

Dax kissed her forehead and held her for a bit. "Now get that cute little ass to the bridge."

"Oh, you noticed," Noora joked. "Good luck. I'll see you later."

"Got our vector set?" Gideon asked.

"Yeah," Noora said, focused on her monitor. She pinged the intercom. "Hey, Dax and Kiwi, just want to check that we're pointed in the right direction and going at the right speed?"

"Roger that, girl, we're good," Kiwi said.

"Yup, we're good." Dax confirmed. *'Vector drive is in the green, and modulated shielding is hot and ready. We'll do a 60-second test flight to make sure everything is*

calibrated. Gideon, all you gotta do is hit the ENGAGE button on your screen."

Jason, sitting off to Gideon's side, whispered, "Hey, what happens if we, like, hit something when we're faster than light?"

Dax chimed in. *"Nothing. Because there's no hitting anything in vector space. We just hope we don't come out of vector space inside a planet or something."*

"And just to be certain," Gideon chimed in, "we're not aiming for a planet, are we, Noora?"

"Oh, no," Noora said. "We're set at a steep angle to the solar system. We're not hitting anything."

"Well then," Gideon said. "If everyone's ready?"

"We're good," Dax said.

"You got it, you flying Scotsman," Kiwi said.

Gideon chuckled.

Noora nodded. "We're good."

"All right then," Gideon said. "So long as there are no objections, hitting ENGAGE in three, two, one—"

The *Isle* lurched for a second, but righted itself. A low-key hum echoed through the ship's hull.

"We looking all right, Dax?" Gideon asked.

"Yeah, uhh, I guess so?"

"What do you mean you *guess* so?"

"I mean, everything looks fine here. First time running the thing."

Gideon looked to Noora, who shrugged her shoulders. "Have 60-seconds gone by yet?" he asked out loud.

"Yeah," Dax said. *"Cutting the drive in three, two—"*

Another lurch went through the ship, and the humming stopped.

Gideon looked to Noora. "Where are we?"

"I mean," Noora said, "it looks good to me, but—"

"Yeah," Dax said over the intercom. *"Readouts are looking good. We covered about 1.9 billion kilometers, so it checks out."*

Gideon breathed a sigh of relief. "Well then," he said. "Noora, take your time to verify that we are still pointed at Lacaille 9352, and set us a course."

"Yes, sir."

"Dax," Gideon continued. "You good to launch again once Noora's set?"

"Oh yeah, we're good to go."

"Wait a minute," Kiwi chimed in. *"Something's not right."*

"What do you mean?" Gideon asked.

"Yeah, what the fuck do you mean?" Dax asked. *"Everything's in the green."*

"No, it's just, hang on," Kiwi said.

Gideon rolled his eyes. "Kiwi, I need a bit more explanation that just *'hang on'.*"

"Wait!" Kiwi said. *"Wait, I got it!"*

Everyone waited for Kiwi's explanation, only to hear *Ride of the Valkyries* echo over the ship's intercom.

Everyone started laughing.

"We're doing this right, kids!" Kiwi said over the intercom, before she started singing along. *"Duh duh duh-duh DAHH duh, duh duh-duh DAHH duh, duh duh-duh DAHH duh, duh duh-duh DAHHHH!"*

Gideon couldn't stop laughing. "Noora, you set?"

"Yup."

"Dax, you set?"

"Yup."

"Bah bah buh-duh DAHH duh, duh duh-dah DAHHHH!!"

"Engaging now," Gideon said, tapping the ENGAGE button.

The *Isle of Skye* shot forward at 112-times the speed of light.

About the Author

Josh cosplays as a motorcyclist even though he's never ridden one. He also writes a weekly Thursday morning newsletter at joshbouchard.substack.com. Originally from nearby Oswego, NY, he now lives near Lake Oswego, OR.

The Isle of Skye is his first published novel. He is currently writing book two.

www.ingramcontent.com/pod-product-compliance
Lightning Source LLC
Chambersburg PA
CBHW061232170626
46809CB00007B/2629